Praise for
IMAGINE A FRIEND

"A powerful and loving ode to lost youth. Quantick captures the emotional turmoil of childhood brilliantly." — Antony Johnston, creator of *Atomic Blonde*

"A soulful fantasy novella about the depths of childhood, full of pain and healing and finally hope. Everyone who ever found or lost a friend will relate." — Paul Cornell, author of *I Walk With Monsters*, the *Lychford* novels, and writer on *Doctor Who*

"I wish this book had been about when I was a teenager! I love this book." — Harry Hill

"David Quantick is a maestro of all forms." — Rev. Richard Coles

"For as long as I've known him, David Quantick has been one of the funniest and most original writers around." — Armando Iannucci

"In *Imagine a Friend*, David Quantick perfectly captures childhood friendships, wonder and sadness. A unique and special tale about the human condition and connection, imagined with equal heart and humour, filled with unforgettable characters." — Harvey Hamer, *Diamond Dimensions Universe* author and *Star Wars Insider* contributor

Also by David Quantick

Fiction

Sparks
The Mule
Go West
All My Colors
Night Train
Ricky's Hand
The Hyena (forthcoming, November 2026)

Short Stories

And Other Stories

IMAGINE A FRIEND

DAVID QUANTICK

Copyright © 2026 David Quantick

All rights reserved. No part of this book may be used or reproduced by any means, graphic, electronic, or mechanical, including photocopying, recording, taping or by any information storage retrieval system without the written permission of the publisher except in the case of brief quotations embodied in critical articles and reviews.

This is a work of fiction. All of the characters, names, incidents, organizations, and dialogue in this novella are either the products of the author's imagination or are used fictitiously.

The views expressed in this work are solely those of the author and do not necessarily reflect the views of the publisher, and the publisher hereby disclaims any responsibility for them.

No part of this work, including the text herein or any cover artwork or interior illustrations, was created through the use of artificial intelligence ("AI") technologies or systems, and no part of this work will be used by the publisher nor may be used or reproduced in any manner by other parties for the purpose of training artificial intelligence technologies or systems.

ISBN: 979-8-9921668-0-4 (trade paper)
ISBN: 979-8-9921668-1-1 (hardcover)
ISBN: 979-8-9921668-2-8 (ePub)
Library of Congress Catalog Number: 2026933282

First printing edition: March 10, 2026
Published by Stars and Sabers Publishing in the United States of America.
Cover Artwork: Kim Herbst
Title Font and Back Cover Layout: Dash Creative
Edited by Jendia Gammon and Gareth L. Powell
Proofreading and Interior Layout by Scarlett R. Algee

https://www.starsandsabers.com/

To Alex and Laurie with love and thanks

IMAGINE A FRIEND

PART ONE—LOUIE

CHAPTER ONE

Imagine a park. A normal kind of park, same as you find in any town—trees and grass, a pond full of ducks and fish, a playground with swings and roundabouts and a sandpit and those weird bouncy elephants on springs—I mean, who puts an elephant on springs? A mad scientist, that's who—and a river running right through the middle, with a bridge over it.

Imagined it yet? A perfectly normal, regular park.

That's my park.

My name is Louie and I pretty much grew up in the park. Every day as far back as I can remember I'd wander—or toddle, or possibly even crawl—over the bridge to the playground. I loved the playground, even the bouncy elephants (I mean, seriously, who looks at an elephant and thinks, you know, that would be better with springs on it?). In fact, my actual first memory is of being in the playground.

I was about three years old. It was a sunny day and all the mums and dads who weren't queuing up for ice creams were sitting on benches, looking at their phones and every so often looking up and shouting GET DOWN FROM THERE YOU'LL BREAK YOUR NECK at their kids.

Did I mention there was a sandpit? There was a sandpit, and I was in it. At the age of three, I loved sand. I liked to play with it, I liked to play in it and I was even convinced the reason I had sandy hair was because sometimes I liked to eat the sand. And I could not get enough of sandpits. I had my own spade and I would sit there for hours, just digging. I had this thing where I'd dig a hole and I'd roll into it. Then I'd roll out again. And then I'd—well, you get the idea. Roll in, roll out. After a while I got bored with rolling and I stopped. I was covered in sand but that was all right with me, so I just sat there, in the sandpit.

And a moment later, she was there.

I heard a "paf" sound, like something small being plonked down in the sandpit, and I looked up to see a girl. She was my age, she had dark hair, and—more importantly—she had a bucket. She sat there, in the sandpit, trying to fill the bucket with sand. I watched her trying to get the sand into the bucket and I remember thinking, *what an amateur.*

She must have seen me staring at her, because she looked right back at me. I realised to my horror that she wasn't looking at me, she was looking at my spade. I clasped the spade to my chest.

She looked at me with pleading eyes.

I shook my head. No way was she getting her hands on my spade.

Her lip started to wobble. A tear formed in her eye. She threw back her head and opened her mouth and—

And I gave her the spade. Just like that. My precious spade, my valuable sand-digging tool: I handed it over to a complete stranger. The girl didn't hesitate. She may not have heard the expression "never look a gift horse in the mouth" but she understood the basic idea. She began to fill her bucket with sand. I looked on with a professional eye. Her shovelling was sloppy but it got the job done. Seconds later the bucket was filled with sand. Pleased with her work, she handed me the bucket.

I emptied it over her head. I don't feel good about that now, but I was three, and I was a boy. The girl sat there, sand in her hair, and looked at me in shock and disbelief. Then she burst into tears. Actually, "burst into tears" doesn't even begin to describe what happened. She wailed. She howled. Water came out of her eyes in salty explosions. You could see where it hit the sand as it made damp dark craters.

I had done something awful and there was only one way I could make it better. I picked up the spade, filled the bucket and tipped it over my own head.

She stopped crying and began sniffling instead.

I filled the bucket and tipped it over my head again.

She wiped a snot bubble from her face.

I shovelled sand into the bucket until it overflowed and this time I *poured* it over my head. My hair was full of sand, my ears were full of sand, and there was sand in my eyes and even in my mouth.

The girl stared at me for a moment. Then she began to laugh. And kept laughing. And kept on laughing. Pointing at me, howling with laughter, rocking back and forth on her backside, and laughing. I had never heard anyone laugh as much as she did.

Eventually she stopped laughing, wiped her eyes with her sandy t-shirt, and stuck her hand out. I was confused at first; then I got it and stuck my own hand out.

We shook hands, like generals after a battle.

"Louie," I said.

"Marcie," she said.

A hand appeared from nowhere and pulled Marcie to her feet. As she left, I waved at her. She waved back, and she was gone.

After that me and Marcie saw each other all the time. I mean, *all* the time. In the park at first—although pretty soon we outgrew the sandpit and started playing on more adventurous stuff, like the roundabout (although neither of us was big enough to push the thing at first) and the swings (not just the kiddie swings either, but the real swings, where the teenagers like to sit for hours, not actually swinging). We even went on the bouncy elephants a few times, and I have to tell you, those things have powerful springs: one time I leaned back too far and nearly got catapulted out of the park. (Needless to say, Marcie just laughed and laughed.)

We got bikes and the world was ours. We cycled around the park, first on stabilisers then later on not. We went up and down the streets, yelling and overtaking each other and trying to crash into the back of the ice cream van. Our parents were fine about it, so long as we were both home in time for tea.

We were always together. Sometimes I'd go to Marcie's and watch cartoons. Sometimes we'd play computer games. But mostly we'd just rush around like crazy people, getting shouted at by grown-ups.

It was the greatest time of my life.

CHAPTER TWO

I was in a hurry and I didn't even hear my mum say, "Hello, Louie," as I ran into the kitchen.

My dad stepped in front of me, a tea towel over his arm. I tried to get in front of him, but he kept blocking my way.

"Your mum said hello," he said, pointedly.

"Sorry," I said, and dodged around him.

"Louie's in too much of a hurry to be polite," said my mum, handing a wet plate to my dad.

"Probably wants to get upstairs and do some more homework," my dad said.

My parents watched me tear around the kitchen, opening cupboards and drawers.

"I'm not *sure*," said my mum slowly, "but I think he's looking for something."

I stopped and turned to look at them both. I had recently come across a new word in a book I'd been reading—"sardonic"—and I hadn't known what it meant but, seeing the expressions on both their faces, I had a pretty good idea.

"You could help me," I told them. "I mean, instead of standing there being all sardonic."

"New word," said my dad approvingly, then:

"We can't help you unless we know what you're looking for."

I could see the logic in this.

"I'm looking for my book," I said.

"Which book?" asked my mum. "And don't say 'the one I was reading.'"

"The one I'm—I mean, *Chocky*," I told her. "I need it because I'm going to Marcie's and—"

The air seemed to stop. I know that sounds weird, but that's literally what happened. One minute I could feel the air in the room, and the next, it was just paused. Like the world had been put on hold.

"Marcie," said my mum, "Again."

"Yeah," I said, "I'm going to go to her house and we're going to watch cartoons and just chill out."

My parents were still on hold. To fill the space, I opened a cupboard. A heap of old comics fell out on my head. And my book.

"Dad! You put my book in the recycling!" I said.

But Dad wasn't listening. He was in the middle of saying something to my mum. It sounded like he was saying—

"What is?" I asked.

Dad shut up instantly.

"What is what?" he said.

"'Imaginary'," I said. "You said something was imaginary."

"No I didn't," my dad said.

Something about the way he said it made me more suspicious.

"What did you say, then?" I asked.

"I—" my dad began, then stopped. He looked at my mum. She rolled her eyes.

"He said 'imagine a friend'," she said.

"Yes!" my dad almost shouted. "I did say that."

My dad often acted in a weird manner—he told jokes that made no sense and said things that apparently people thought were funny when he was a kid—but right now he was acting more strangely than usual.

"Why?" I asked.

"Why what?" my dad said.

His eyes were full of panic and he kept using them to look at my mum, who clearly had no desire to be involved in whatever was going on.

"Why," I said slowly, in case he truly had lost his mind, "why did you say, 'imagine a friend'?"

"Because of Marcie!" my dad said. "I meant, imagine! A friend like her! She's great."

He looked to my mother for support but she had turned her back on him. We could still see her shaking her head, though.

I looked at the kitchen clock.

"I'm late," I said. I grabbed the book and left.

As I headed for the door I could hear my mum say:

"Michael, any time you want to give up talking, let me know, OK?"

I left the house and walked down the street. It was a warm day and Ali the ice cream man had his van parked at the end of the road. I liked Ali. Some people said he was weird because he was always out in his van, whatever the weather, but I didn't see what was wrong with that. Ali was a tryer and that was fine by me.

"Hi Louie," said Ali, leaning out the little window. He had a very deep voice. "Are you in the mood for an ice cream?"

Ali always talked like this. It was like he and my dad went to the same Let's Talk Like Weirdos class.

"No thanks, Ali," I said. "I'm on my way to Marcie's."

Ali looked puzzled for a second then said: "Oh right. Your *friend.*"

He didn't say it in an unpleasant way, but it sounded like how my dad had said the word "friend" earlier.

"Yeah," I said. "She's my best friend."

"Well, good luck, kid," Ali said.

Which was another weird thing to say.

I walked through the park and over the bridge to get to Marcie's house, which was on the very far side of the park (when I pointed this out to her one day, she said, "No. *You* live on the very far side of the park. *I* live near it." I didn't argue the point: when Marcie got an idea in her head, it was hard to get it out again).

The park was empty that morning, and as I crossed the bridge it began to rain, so I ran.

I was in Marcie's room. I had my book and she was reading an old Calvin and Hobbes collection that had belonged to her dad. There was a tray on the floor with sandwich crusts and empty cola bottles.

I closed the book and looked out the window. The sky was full of drab-looking clouds. I looked around the room. Marcie's collection of rainbow ponies stared back at me, glassy-eyed from years imprisoned on her shelves.

"I'm bored," I said.

Marcie didn't even look up from her book.

"Not my fault," she said.

"It sort of is," I said, "Since you're just lying there reading a book."

"Says the boy just lying there reading a book," Marcie replied.

Then she grinned.

"Hey, Louie?"

"What?" I asked.

Suddenly Marcie was holding her Nerf gun.

"Run," she said, and fired.

There was nowhere to run, so I leapt. I jumped onto the bed as she reloaded. Marcie fired again and her shot nearly clipped me as I rolled across the floor. Her third shot hit the shelf and ponies went everywhere.

We were silent for a second, taking in the devastation. Then Marcie flopped onto her back and laughed. I joined in. We were laughing so much we didn't even hear the door open and Laura come in. Laura was here because Marcie's mum and dad were out trying to, as Marcie said, "fix things," whatever that meant, and she was Marcie's babysitter. She was sixteen or something and she had a really short temper, but she mostly stayed downstairs watching stupid dating shows where grown-ups with shiny skin sat in a swimming pool and talked about their eyebrows.

Laura had a look on her face, bored and annoyed at the same time. She looked round the room.

"Keep it down," she told Marcie, "or I'll tell your mum and dad you were acting up."

And she left.

Marcie was silent. She sat sort of folded over.

"Are you all—" I began.

WHOMP! A Nerf ball hit me in the face.

"You snooze, you lose," said Marcie.

I felt my nose.

"I think it's broken," I said.

"I shot you with a foam ball," said Marcie. "I think you'll be fine."

I looked at the clock on her wall. There was a picture of a rainbow pony on it and the hands of the clock were the pony's front legs. Right now one leg was sticking up and the other was pointing down: it looked like the pony was trying to measure something with its hooves.

"Six o'clock!" I said. "I'm late for my tea."

"Bye," said Marcie, without looking up from her book.

I raced home through the park. It was still raining but as I crossed the bridge the sun came out again. I nearly ran into Ali's ice cream van as he reversed out into the road, and I did run into my dad as he opened the front door the exact same moment as I came in.

"Dinner's on the table," he said.

"You're right, it is," I said as I sat down.

He pretended to hit me.

"Can we just eat in peace and quiet?" asked my mum.

"That's up to him," my dad and I said in unison.

My mum sighed and began to eat.

After dinner, as I was loading the dishwasher, my mum came up behind me and put her arms round me like a human backpack.

"Stop it," I said. "I've got a frying pan and I'm not afraid to use it."

"Frying pans don't go in the dishwasher," she said.

"Always in mum mode," I replied, but I put the pan back on the side.

"Are you all right, Louie?" my mum asked.

I turned to face her, which was hard because I was still entangled in her arms.

"I'm fine," I said. "Why?"

It felt like I was using that word a lot today.

"Because you're either in your room or you're with your friend," she said. She said the word *friend* the way Dad and Ali had.

"That's OK, isn't it?" I replied. "I mean, when I'm in my room I'm not hatching plots to blow up the world, and when I'm with *Marcie*—that's my friend's name, by the way," I added sarcastically, "I'm, you know, hanging out."

My mum finally released me from her octopus grip, but only so she could step back and look at me.

"It's just you're getting older," she said. "You're not a little kid anymore. And you're still spending a lot of time with Marcie."

I had no idea where this conversation was going, but I wasn't enjoying it.

"She's my friend, mum," I said. "My best friend."

Mum must have heard something in my voice because she stepped back. There was concern in her eyes: and then she said something *really* weird.

"I just don't want you to get hurt, that's all."

CHAPTER THREE

When you're a kid you've got too much to think about—homework, television, food, running around—without wondering what your parents are talking about as well. Also adults have this way of one minute being really uncomfortably close to you, like being in your face and on your case, and the next minute—well, doing what my mum did. Stepping back and looking at you like an alien object they've never seen before.

So I didn't think about what my mum said at all. Not consciously, anyway.

One day I was in the park with Marcie—not in the playground, that was for kids—but in the café.

"You want a cola?" she asked.

"It's OK, I'll get them," I said.

She laughed.

"Right," she said.

"What?" I replied.

"Nothing," said Marcie. "It's just—you *never* have any money."

I tried to look angry but instead I grinned, because it was true. Whenever I met up with Marcie and I tried to pay for something, I never seemed to have any cash on me. My mum and dad gave me pocket money, but whenever I went out, my pockets were empty.

A lesser person would have thought I was doing it deliberately, but Marcie was not a lesser person.

"I'll get them," she said.

"Thanks," I said. "Can you get some crisps, too?"

She gave me a *very* strong look.

We sat there, our faces sticky with cola and salty with crisps. It was a nice day, cloudless and warm.

"Better get back," said Marcie.

She was getting up to leave when I said:

"Hey Marcie?"
She stopped fastening up her backpack.
"What?"
I felt uncomfortable.
"What?" she repeated.
"You think—you think we'll always be friends?"
Marcie sat down again. She gave me a long look, like my mum did. Like she was—new word—*appraising* me.
"Wow," she said. "What brought that on?"
I shrugged my shoulders (obviously—what else could I shrug? My ears?).
"I don't know," I said. "Lately I've been feeling—"
"Crazy? Annoying?"
I thought for a moment.
"Discombobulated," I said.
"Discomwhat?" said Marcie.
"Discombobulated."
"That's not a word," Marcie said.
"It is! It's my new word of the week."
Marcie made a face.
"OK," she said. "But you still haven't answered my question."
I looked at the ground.
"Sometimes thoughts just come into my head," I told her. "And I don't know what to do with them, so I just say them."
"I see," said Marcie. "Well, perhaps this—"
She reached into her backpack and pulled out her Nerf gun.
"—will help?" she said.
"What? No!" I shouted. "How is that going to help?"
But Marcie had already taken aim. I jumped out of my seat and ran.

When I finally stopped running, there was no sign of Marcie, so I guessed that she'd gone home. I didn't feel any safer: if there was one thing more dangerous than Marcie with a Nerf gun, it was Marcie with a Nerf gun and unfinished business.

I walked back through town, carefully checking every side street and doorway as I went.

It was getting darker now and the shops were closing. I slowed my pace, and that was when I noticed my laces were undone. I bent down and came face to face with a face. I was looking right into the eyes of a stuffed cat. Well, not an actual stuffed cat, but a small—a very small—toy cat. It was in the window of a toy shop and it had big round brown eyes that reminded me of something, or rather someone—it looked, to me, like Marcie.

I looked in my pocket and discovered I did, in fact, have some money. Three minutes later, I was the owner of a very small stuffed cat.

The next day I met Marcie in the park and gave her the cat. If I had expected her to be excited and dance round and hug me, then I was disappointed. She took the cat and stared at it, for a really long time. Then she said:

"OK, this is weird."

I wanted to take it back. I wanted to run out of the park and throw the stupid cat into the sun. I heard myself gabbling:

"Is it too much? It just—I don't know—it reminded me of you. Because you're so cool and cat-like."

By rights, Marcie should have put a bag over my head or glued my lips together: at this point I would have welcomed it. Instead she said.

"No, that's not weird. *This* is."

And she handed me something small and gift-wrapped.

I tore off the wrapping. Inside the paper was a very small toy stuffed dog. It was brown with bright blue eyes.

"Wow," I said. "That is—"

I couldn't think of the right word. I couldn't even think of the wrong word.

"There was something about it made me think of you," said Marcie. She looked a bit embarrassed.

"Did it make you think of me because it's cool?" I asked.

Marcie gave me one of her looks. Then she smiled.

"Cool—and dog-like," she said.

I nodded.

"I'll take that," I said.

I hugged her. Just like that. Well, I started a hug—I moved forwards with my arms apart, and Marcie, instead of punching me in the chest or running backwards in the opposite direction as quickly as she could, stepped into my arms and hugged me back.

We separated.

"OK, dog boy," said Marcie, "Got to go."

And it was like she was never there.

I walked back over the bridge. My street was quiet except for the far-off ring of bells which, as I stood there, seemed to be getting nearer. I looked up to see Ali's van coming down the road.

Ali parked and leaned out of the serving window.

"Hi Louie!" he called. "You want an ice cream?"

"It's dinner time!" I said.

Ali smiled.

"Ice cream is a meal!" he said.

"It really isn't," I said.

"Worth a try," said Ali. He watched as I walked down the road to my house.

When I got in, my mum and dad were making dinner.

"What's that you've got there?" my dad said, nodding at the stuffed toy in my hand.

"It's a dog," I said. "A present from Marcie."

There was an odd silence. My mum put down the glass she was holding.

"Marcie bought you a present?" she asked.

I saw her look at my dad.

I didn't know people couldn't buy me presents without your permission, I wanted to say. I didn't, though.

"It's a dog," I said. "He doesn't have a name yet but I was thinking 'Mister Dog'."

"I like it," said my dad. "Accurate. I mean, unless it's a lady dog, in which case."

"Michael," my mum said.

"Just saying," said my dad, and stopped talking.

I had no idea what was going on, which was probably why I got nervous and started babbling.

"Honestly, it's crazy," I said. "Because she got me this and I got her—a cat!"

They both looked at me.

"A real cat?" asked my dad. My mum rolled her eyes.

"No occasion too serious for a joke," she said,

"It's a dad joke," said my dad. "And I'm a dad. I can't help it."

"You got that right," my mum said. She handed him a plate.

"Serve up," she said.

Some expressions are confusing and the most confusing one I can think of is "there was an atmosphere." Because if you're on an alien planet, it's a good thing because it means you can take off your space helmet and breathe. But if you're in a dining room on Earth with your parents, and there's an atmosphere, then it's a bad thing. You feel like you can't breathe and you wish you had a space helmet on.

These were the thoughts running through my mind as I watched Dad go through his pasta looking for mushrooms. He didn't like them, but that didn't stop my mum putting them in his pasta, because she said it was too much effort to leave them out otherwise. Anyway, my dad was jabbing mushrooms and putting them on a side plate and my mum was looking worried—or at least looking like she was trying not to look worried, which was somehow worse. Nobody was talking but everyone looked like they were thinking of something to say, and whatever it was, it wasn't going to be about mushrooms.

And I wished I was wearing a space helmet.

After a while, my dad could take it no longer.

"So, Louie," he said. "What did you do today?"

I held up Mister Dog.

"Apart from get a dog," said my dad.

"Well," I began. "I went round to Marcie's to see if she wanted to come out, but she was out."

"OK," my dad said, "Then—"

"So I sat on her doorstep and waited until she got back," I said. "And finally she came home. She'd been shopping with her mum. Oh!" I suddenly realised something. "Maybe that's when she got me the dog."

"Did you—" my mum began, but I was hitting my stride.

"Anyway, she told her mum she was going to the park, so we went off together and we just—I don't know—chilled out. There are some new chicks in the park, I think they're goslings but Marcie says they're ducklings. Then we sat on a bench for a while—"

I paused to take in a breath or two. My mum saw her opportunity.

"Did you do anything else today, Louie?" she asked.

"Yeah, we went to—"

"I mean," she said sort of firmly, "anything that didn't involve Marcie?"

I thought for a moment. Finally I said:

"I came home and watched Dad pick things out of his pasta."

My dad sighed. Maybe he was thinking about the mushrooms again. Then he said:

"Son. Do you ever—"

My mum interrupted him. She had a really serious expression on her face.

"Michael," she said, "is now the time?"

I said, "Time for what?"

"Nothing," said my dad. He shot my mum a look that I did not get at all.

"I think that what your dad means..." my mum began.

"What he *means*?" repeated my dad.

"Michael," said my mum, "If we're going to do this now, let me do it."

"*Fine*," said my dad, and folded his arms. He was clearly in a huff, his favourite kind where he acted like nobody ever let him do things his way.

My mum took both my hands. That was how I knew it was serious. Holding both my hands meant she could look right into my eyes and also I couldn't run away.

"Louie," she said. "Sweetheart."

I instantly felt more nervous.

"Dad's mushrooms are getting cold," I said. Nobody laughed.

My mum let go my hands.

"You do it," she told my dad.

"Do *what*?" I almost shouted.

My dad unfolded his arms. I folded mine, just in case he was going for the hands again.

"Louie," he said. "We know you like Marcie."

"Like her? She's my best friend," I said.

"It's just—" My dad stopped. "It's just you're getting older and you know, soon you'll want other friends."

"No I won't!" I said. "Me and Marcie don't need other friends! When we're together it's—it's like there's nobody else in the world!"

I could hear someone shouting and realised it was me.

My mum leaned over.

"What your dad is trying to say—" she began.

"Trying?" huffed my dad, and folded his arms again.

"Be quiet, Mike," said my mum.

"Yeah, be quiet Dad," I said.

"What your dad means is that people change, Louie. They get older, they move on in their lives. They move away from each other."

"Move away?" I asked, startled. "Are we moving house? Because I need to tell Marcie—"

"Good work, Sheila," my dad said. To me he said, "No son, we're not moving. What your mother is *trying* to say is that one day soon—really soon—you and Marcie are going to outgrow each other."

Dad's words sank in. The way a huge sword sinks into someone's heart when you run them through with it.

"Not me!" I said, loudly. "I'm going to be friends with Marcie for LIFE!"

And I got up, knocking my chair over, and left the room.

"Good talk," Mum said to Dad.

I was sitting on a swing in the playground with Dog. I called him Dog now because Mister Dog sounded like a name a kid would give a dog. I didn't feel like I was a kid anymore. I mean, yes, I was on a swing, but I wasn't swinging. That was the big difference: little kids swing on the swings, but older kids sit on them.

I was sitting on the swing with Dog because I was waiting for Marcie. Not that I had arranged to meet her exactly. I hadn't seen her for a few days, maybe longer. She hadn't been in the park lately and the one or two (all right, maybe three) times I'd been to her house I'd heard raised voices inside and I had gone home rather than disturb anyone. My mum and dad argued from time to time but Marcie's parents argued a *lot*.

So there I was, sitting on the swing with Dog. I wasn't playing with him or anything like that, but sometimes when there was no-one else around, I would talk to him. It sounds silly but because he had the same eyes as Marcie I felt like he would be a good listener.

Right now Dog and me were scanning the park to see if Marcie was anywhere around.

"No sign of her yet," I told Dog. He said nothing. Then:

"Dog! Is that—?"

It was. Marcie walking on her own, on the other side of the lake (there was a small ornamental lake just a few steps from the playground: my dad called it the Fake Lake but no-one else did). We watched as Marcie walked towards a bench and sat down on it.

Obviously she hadn't seen us, I mean me (sorry, Dog). I got up and walked round the Fake Lake to Marcie's bench.

When I got there, she had the cat I'd given her in her hand and she was just sitting there, looking down at the ground.

"Hi," I said, but she didn't reply.

I sat down next to her. She still didn't look up.

"OK," I said, good-naturedly, "If you don't want to talk to me, maybe you'll talk to Dog."

I waved Dog under her nose.

"Hi Marcie," I said in a squeaky voice.

Nothing.

"Are you all right?" I asked her.

Marcie didn't look up—she was now looking quite intensely at her toy cat—but she did let out a long sigh.

"My—" she began, and stopped. I realised with a shock that she was crying.

"Marcie," I said. I moved closer to her on the bench, but she was still focussed on the toy cat.

"My dad left today," she said.

"No, what? Marcie, that's awful," I said. "I can't imagine how you must feel. I'm so sorry."

Marcie wiped her eyes. Then she said:

"It's just me and mum now, Mister Cat."

I tried not to take offence at this in the circumstances.

"Hey," I said, in a good-humoured way. "One—*Mister Cat*? Nice name. And two—"

I looked at her tear-stained face. She was so unhappy that at that moment I would have done anything for her.

"Two," I said, "It's not just you and your mum, Marcie, there's—"

Marcie forced a smile.

"That's right," she said. "I forgot you. You're always there for me."

"I am," I said.

"—Mister Cat."

And she held the tiny cat close to her and hugged it.

I sat bolt upright.

"What?" I said, "Marcie, is this a joke? Are you pranking me? Because I realise you're having a bad day—a very bad day—but it's not funny."

Marcie ignored me.

"I feel like there's something I'm supposed to be doing today," she told Mister Cat.

I couldn't take this much longer.

"Yes!" I shouted. "There is something you're supposed to be doing today! Seeing *me*. Marcie, you're supposed to be—"

In my outrage, I waved my hand in front of her face.

She didn't flinch. She didn't even blink.

"—seeing me," I said.

Then I said:

"You can't see me."

It was true. Marcie couldn't see me. She couldn't hear me. It was like I wasn't there.

I stood in front of her. She didn't react. I leaned in, so our noses were nearly touching.

Nothing.

It was as if I wasn't there.

We stayed like that for a while, me standing in front of Marcie, and Marcie looking at her toy cat. I didn't know what to do: what could I do? I could have pinched her, I suppose, and part of me wanted to; but another part of me was scared to.

What if I couldn't pinch her? What if I couldn't touch her?

What if my hand passed right through her?

Eventually Marcie said:

"I'd better get home, Mister Cat. Mum needs us."

And she got up and left.

I walked after her.

"Marcie!" I shouted, right in her ear. "Marcie, it's me, Louie!"

She walked on and it felt like she was walking away from me deliberately.

I stopped following her. What was the point? I could stand in front of her if I liked and she'd probably just walk right through me. I was a ghost to her. Not even that: people can see ghosts.

I was standing by a bench, so I sat down on it.

When I was a little kid, I was always making friendships with other kids that lasted about a week. It was no big deal: you'd be friends with someone, then you'd have a massive argument about a toy or something, and you'd be mortal enemies. Or you'd be absolute total best friends for ever, ever, *ever*, with some kid on Monday morning, and on Tuesday afternoon you'd be bored with them and never want to see them again. So I understood that friendships don't always last.

And I understood that people change. They grow out of each other, if you know what I mean. One day you and your best friend are inseparable because you both like the same toys and the same games: the next you're no longer into those same things, and you drift apart. It's natural, it's just what happens. You feel sad for a while, then you meet new people who share your interests, and life goes on.

But I had never experienced what just happened with Marcie.

I could have taken being blanked by her (maybe). I would even have been OK (eventually) if she'd told me she never wanted to see me again. I might even have got over it one day if Marcie had just screamed in my face that I was a horrible person and she hoped I fell into an active volcano just as it erupted.

What I couldn't take was being invisible to her. And I do mean "invisible." Because, incredible as it may seem, that was exactly what had just happened. It wasn't that she was pretending not to see me, like people sometimes do: and she wasn't ignoring me either. She literally could not see me. It wasn't "like" I wasn't there: *I wasn't there.*

I had no idea how this could have happened. I mean, I could see her. And the day before she could see me, and the day before that and— I stopped. I was crying. Fortunately it was getting dark and there was nobody around to see me.

Which was good, because even if they couldn't see me, they could have heard me. I was bawling my eyes out. I hadn't cried like this since I was little and I had come off my bike and scraped my knees. I remember Marcie had come up and put her arm round me and—

Enough, I thought. Right now the one thing I didn't need was happy memories. But then right now the only thing I needed couldn't see me. At all.

I got off the bench and began to walk home.

CHAPTER FOUR

I walked through the park past the playground towards the bridge. Then I stopped.

I must have crossed the bridge nearly every single day of my life: after all, I'd been coming here nearly every single day of my life. And I'd been to the park so often that I'd never really looked at it. I mean, it was a park: and once you've seen one park, you've pretty much seen them all. Trees, ducks, benches, a playground: put them together and there it is, a park.

But I'd never really looked at the *details* before. Like, there was a big noticeboard by the Fake Lake, with a map of the whole park on it, and the words YOU ARE HERE. Marcie and I used to think that was hilarious. I mean, where else are you but here? (Except now I wasn't here, at least in Marcie's eyes.)

There were benches with names on (MUM LOVED IT HERE), stones with inscriptions (ALDERMAN BARTLETT PLANTED THIS OAK), little plaques under bushes (TO COMMEMORATE THE QUEEN'S DIAMOND JUBILEE) and even name tags on the trees, in case you wanted to impress someone by asking them, "Hey! Isn't that a Canadian Silver Birch?"

And, as I neared the bridge, I saw something else for the first time. The bridge had always been festooned (good word) with what I thought were tiny flags, or banners. They were small and faded and I always assumed that they'd been put up for some party or event years ago and just left there. But as I got nearer, I saw what they really were for the first time.

They were photographs. And there were hundreds of them—I'm not exaggerating when I say that there were so many photos that they were hung on the side of the bridge in layers, the newest on top and the oldest buried underneath. Most of the photographs were small; some of them were big. Most were old-fashioned snaps like you see stuffed in a drawer, some were portraits like a professional photographer might take, and a lot were printed on paper from computers or phones. The oldest were so faded you could hardly see what was in them, and the newest were headed that way, but they all had one thing in common: in every photo—almost every photo, anyway—there were two kids. Big kids and little kids, girls and boys, kids in glasses and kids in sports kit, kids smiling and kids frowning: but always in pairs. And you could tell from the expressions on their faces that these kids were friends—and not just friends, but best friends in the world ever.

I didn't understand it, not then anyway, but there was something about the sheer amount of all these photos that made me feel sad and happy all at the same time. Normally when you see pictures of people you don't know, you're interested for about two seconds and then you get bored because you don't know them and you don't really care—but this was different. The effect of seeing all these photos of kids, these hundreds of kids, all smiling (mostly), all with their best friends ever, was enormous.

All that friendship.

It should have made me feel good.

Instead, it just made me feel lonelier than ever.

I walked down my road.

Ali's ice cream van was parked across from my house. As soon as he saw me coming, he switched on the chimes.

I kept walking.

Ali turned off the chimes and as I opened my front door, I could hear them slow down. They sounded as sad as I did.

When I came in, my parents were in the kitchen dancing to the radio. They did that from time to time, and sometimes they even grabbed me and made me join in.

Not today, though. My mum took one look at me and turned the radio off.

"Hey!" said my dad. "I was—"

He stopped. He'd seen my face too.

"Oh no," he said. "It happened."

Then both he and my mum knelt down and put their arms round me.

I thought I'd cried before, but that was nothing. Right now, with both my mum and my dad holding me, I totally lost it. I wasn't crying, I wasn't even bawling, I was *yowling*. I must have sounded like a wolf howling at the moon or at the very least a dog trapped in a well. My parents didn't say anything while I howled. They just held on to me, like I would have flown out the window otherwise.

I don't know how long the three of us were there but after a while—a long while—I stopped howling and started to gulp, like I was trying to drink my own tears. Then the gulping turned to sniffing, and it was quiet again. Until my dad said:

"Can I get up now? I think something's happened to my knee."

"Michael!" said my mum, disapprovingly.

I smiled at them. I could barely see them through the haze of tears.

"It's OK," I said. "I've stopped now."

A second later, like a tidal wave, I started crying again.

Finally, I stopped. My dad went to get kitchen roll ("Not the whole roll, Michael! A couple of pieces is fine!"), my mum made tea with honey in it, and we sat down at the kitchen table to drink the tea, which was more like honey with tea in it.

After a while I said:

"Dad—what did you mean when you said, 'it happened'?"

He looked at me with a vague expression on his face.

"Did I say that? Ow!"

The "ow!" was because my mum had just punched him in the arm.

She turned and looked at me. The expression on her face was new to me: it was sadness and love, all together.

"She couldn't see you, could she?" asked my mum. "Marcie—she couldn't see you or hear you, and it was like you weren't there."

I nodded. I tried to swallow, but my throat was too dry. A glass of water appeared from nowhere and my dad smiled at me.

There was something I needed to say, something I had to ask. I was terrified to let the words leave my mouth, but I had to do it.

"Mum, Dad," I said, looking from one to the other, "Am I a ghost?"

My mum smiled, and it was the saddest, sweetest smile in the world.

"No, sweetie," she said. "You're not a ghost. You're a living boy."

My dad nodded. "Yep. As real as anyone in this or any other world."

I frowned.

"Then—is *Marcie* a ghost?"

Dad looked at Mum and she nodded. He took a deep breath and said:

"Son, do you know what an invisible friend is?"

I nodded. It was a weird question but at least I knew the answer.

"'Course I do," I said. "It's what kids have when they don't have any other friends. Like a friend that only they can see, except the reason only they can see them is because the friend isn't real. They're an *imaginary friend*."

As I said the word, I could hear an echo in my head.

My dad saying the words:

"Imagine a friend…"

Except that wasn't what he said. That was what he told me he said. What he really said was what I'd just said.

"Imaginary friend."

CHAPTER FIVE

Time stopped. Everything stopped. I swear I could hear my own blood pulsing in my veins.

"Wait," I said. "Are you saying that—that Marcie was my imaginary friend?"

My mum and dad were silent, like they were waiting for me to work something out. Like they wanted me to *think*.

So I thought.

"But that doesn't make sense," I said. "Because if she was my imaginary friend, that would have meant that I was the only person who could see her. And—"

And everyone could see her, I said in my head.

The people in the café who sold us crisps and colas.

Laura the awful babysitter.

Everyone.

There was no doubt about it: Marcie was real.

She was my best friend and she was real.

I was her best friend and—

"No," I said.

It was like I had been struck by my own personal bolt of lightning.

"No!" I said again, louder, then I shouted:

"NO!"

My mum took my hand. So did my dad. I wasn't a kid anymore but I let them.

"You mean," I said, and I stopped.

They waited.

"You mean *I'm* the imaginary friend?" I said.

My parents looked at me, and there was so much love in their eyes.

"We prefer the term 'invisible friend'," said my mum. "Because the way we see it, we're not imaginary. They just can't see us anymore."

"Really?" said my dad. "I thought it was 'incredible friend.' Because we're, you know, incredible."

"Stop talking now," said my mum.

"Right you are," said my dad.

"Wait," I said. "You said 'we'."

"Yes I did," my dad replied.

"Does that mean that you're—that both of you are—"

My mum and dad nodded.

"Sure does," said my dad. "At least, we were."

"We all are," said my mum. "You, me, your dad, everyone."

"What?" I said, totally confused now. "How? When?"

"When we were kids, like you," my dad said. "All of us. We were kids and we had friends, just like you and Marcie. Even Ali the ice cream man."

I tried to picture Ali as a kid, sitting on a bench with another kid.

"I don't believe this," I said.

I looked at Mum.

"You were an imaginary friend?" I asked. "*Dad* was an imaginary friend?"

"Yes," my mum said.

"And you had—real friends? Like best friends?"

My Dad nodded. His expression was sad and serious now and I realised he was remembering.

"Her name was Alice," he said. "We did everything together. Went on bike rides, climbed trees, we even learned to swim together. The swim teacher couldn't see me, but I didn't know that. I was just doing what Alice did. Of course I was. She was my best friend in the world, ever."

I suddenly realised I wasn't seeing Dad as he was now—my dad, a grown-up who told terrible jokes and knew how to make lasagne—but as he was years ago, a boy my age who had a friend he thought would be there for ever.

"I remember the day it happened," said my dad. "We were in her garden playing football. Her mum came out and called her in for tea. And she just turned and went without saying a word to me.

"I called out her name, but she didn't hear. I shouted 'ALICE!' at the top of my voice. She did stop, then. She turned her head, like she'd heard something in the far distance. Then she shook it off and went inside. And that was it. She never even said goodbye."

My mum took my dad's hand.

"They never say goodbye," she told me. "That's the worst part."

My dad got up.

"I'm going to make some more tea," he said.

"Make sure there's biscuits," my mum told him. Then she looked at me and said:

"It was the same for me."

I said, "Who was your—"

I couldn't say *real friend*.

"Who was your friend?" I finished.

My mum smiled, or at least, she tried to.

"His name was Joey," she said. "He was a quiet kid. He didn't like to go out, so mostly we sat in his room and played Super Mario Kart."

I tried to imagine my mum, racing a tiny car or mowing down zombies with a machine gun.

"You played video games?" I asked.

"Well, Joey played and I watched," said my mum. "I always wondered why it was never my turn."

Dad put down three mugs and a plate of biscuits.

"We've all been there, kid," he said. "We all had someone who one minute was our best friend for ever and the next—pff. Gone."

I ate a biscuit. It tasted real.

But how would I know what 'real' was? I thought. Was this a dream? Right then it felt more like a nightmare.

"I don't understand any of this," I told my parents. "It doesn't make sense. They're real and we're—not."

"We're real," said my mum firmly. "As real as they are. Just not—real to them. Anymore."

"Why?" I asked, and I could hear the panic in my voice. "How come one minute we're there and the next we're not? It doesn't make any sense."

My dad shrugged. Like there wasn't anything he could do about it. Which, I suppose, there wasn't.

"That's just the way it is, Louie," he said. "I think we're only there—for them—when they need us."

"And they do need us," said my mum. "Our worlds may look the same, but they're very different."

I must have looked confused, because my dad said:

"There's no dark here in our world, Louie. But their world— Marcie's world—is a very dark place sometimes."

I didn't understand what he meant by "Marcie's world." Surely Marcie's world was the same as my world? But then I didn't understand hardly anything they were saying.

"But she's my friend!" I said. "And she needs me! Her dad just walked out!"

"I'm sorry, Louie," said my dad. "It happens to everyone. The day comes when we all cross the bridge for the last time."

"The bridge?" I asked. "You mean the bridge to the park?"

I could see myself now, on the bridge, with the pictures that I thought were banners. The bridge between my side of the park and Marcie's side of the park.

Two sides, connected by one bridge.

My mum nodded.

"That's the bridge to their world," she said. "I mean, it's not the only bridge, but yes."

I stood up.

"I want to go back," I said.

"You can't go back, sweetheart," said my mum.

"Why not?" I asked. I was getting angry again. All these new facts—all these new ideas—and now it seemed there was also a whole set of new rules.

"Why not?" I asked. "The bridge is still there, right? I can still cross it. So I can go back."

"It doesn't work like that, son," said my dad.

"I don't care!" I said. "Even if she can't see me, I'll still be able to see her. I could still—"

I didn't know what I could still do. Maybe nothing: but it didn't matter. I could still be with Marcie. Maybe I could protect her somehow. And maybe one day she'd be able to see me again.

My mum must have seen what I was thinking, because she said:

"It doesn't matter if they can see us or not. If we stay in their world and they no longer believe in us, we start to fade away. Until we really *are* ghosts."

I stared at her, willing her to say it wasn't true. But she just looked at me sadly.

My dad nodded.

"That's just the—"

"Don't say 'that's just the way it is'!" I shouted at him. "Because the way it is is stupid! And it's—it's not *right*."

My dad let out the world's longest sigh.

"You're right," he said. "It's not right. One day you cross the bridge, and you're happy and joyful because you're going to see your best friend again. And the next, you're coming back over the same bridge with your heart ripped out."

"Michael," said my mum. "You could try and make it sound less—final."

"Sorry," said my dad.

He looked so unhappy that I found myself putting my arm around him.

"Don't worry, dad," I told him. "I get it. Because that's exactly how I feel. And"—now it was my turn to let out the world's longest sigh—"I suppose I'll feel like this forever."

To my surprise, my mum punched my arm.

"No," she said, firmly. "No, you won't, Louie. Because time heals. You may not feel it, but it does, slowly. I got over Joey, your dad got over Alice. And we met each other. I started a new life."

"And so did I," said my dad.

He took my mother's hand.

"With someone who could actually see me," he said.

They looked at each other in a way I really, really hoped someone would look at me one day. Like friends, only different, and more so.

"Someone who *really* sees me," he said.

"All right, don't overdo it," said my mum, smiling.

"Louie, you'll get over it," said my dad. "It hurts now, but you will get over it."

"Like you did?" I asked him.

My dad was smiling, but there was something under the smile.

"Sure," he said.

He patted my mum's hand.

"Absolutely," he said.

CHAPTER SIX

There's a joke my dad told me once. Like most of my dad's jokes, it was really long and it wasn't funny, but here it is anyway.

Two kids are sitting in the park. Let's call them Bill and Ben. Bill's looking at his phone when suddenly he says, "Oh no!"

Ben says, "What's wrong?" and Bill says, "Look at this!" and shows him his phone. There's a headline on the screen: THE END OF THE WORLD.

Bill says, "According to this, a giant asteroid's going to hit the earth and destroy half the planet."

"Oh no!" says Ben, "That's terrible!"

"And not only that," says Bill, "But there's going to be an alien invasion and any surviving humans will be taken to a far-off galaxy and made to work in the uranium mines!"

"Oh no!" says Ben again.

"Not only *that*," says Bill, "but it's all going to happen on Saturday."

Ben looks at him in horror.

"Saturday!" he says.

"I know!" says Bill. "We don't even get the day off school!"

Hilarious, right? I mean, I bet the police are still trying to find the point of that joke. I expect archaeologists are still looking for the exact ten second time period when that joke was funny. But the odd thing about my dad's terrible joke is this: it was a pretty good description of how I was feeling.

My life had been blown to pieces, but I still had to go on living it. My world had been turned upside down, but I was still here. Everything I knew, or rather thought I knew, everything I believed, everything I'd assumed was true—it had all been blown up in a moment, leaving me behind.

You know those movies where somebody wakes up and they're trapped in a repeat of the same day on a loop, over and over again? Everything they do, they already did yesterday, and they're going to do it again today, and they're going to do it again tomorrow, and the day after that, and the day after the day after that, until they "learn to love themselves" or "embrace their demons" or just apologise to a girl for being a jackass. That's how the next few months felt for me.

Every day I got up, ate something, said goodbye to my parents, walked down the street, said hello to Ali the ice cream man (who for some reason was now selling ice creams in our street all the year round), and walked to school. And at the end of school, I did it all again, except in reverse. Every day was the same, just like the movies, except I didn't get to love myself or embrace any demons (and how can you apologise to a girl who can't see you?).

The world had ended, but I still had to go to school. Life goes on.

Life went on. Spring came, and it was a good one. The days were longer and the nights were shorter. Then one day, my dad looked up from his breakfast and said:

"There's a funfair coming to town and I think we should go."

My mum and I looked at him in shared disbelief.

"A funfair?" said my mum. "Like with roundabouts and helter skelters and bumper cars?"

"Yes," said my dad, apparently not hearing the ironic tone in her voice. "I thought it might be fun. Take Louie out of his, you know. Shell."

I got it.

"Dad," I said. "I'm fine. I'm not in my shell."

"He's fine," my mum said.

"I am," I said. And I meant it.

"All right then," said my dad. He picked up his newspaper (my dad was the last man in the world to read newspapers at breakfast time: I think he had them privately printed) and tried to not look hurt.

I looked at my mum. She nodded.

"Actually," I said. "I'd love to go to a funfair. I haven't been on the bumper cars since forever."

My dad put down his newspaper. His expression was both excited and hopeful.

"Really?" he asked. He looked at my mum.

"Really?" he said. "Because it might be too late to get tickets—"

My mum gave him a look. It was quite an affectionate look.

"You bought tickets already, didn't you?" she said.

My dad looked sheepish.

"Maybe," he said.

I wasn't kidding about the bumper cars. I loved them when I was a kid, even when I was too small to drive them and I used to sit next to my dad and shout directions at him. The only trouble was, my dad drove like a little old grandpa, carefully avoiding all the other cars and frequently going the wrong way. I was always shouting LEFT! at him when he was going right, and vice versa. I didn't mind too much because we always ended up slamming into another car, and that was fun: but when I was finally big enough to drive my own bumper car, it was a lot better.

I raced round the track, dodging and bumping, being careful not to ram any very small kids (or any very big kids) and when the power went off, jumped out of my car like a boss while my mum applauded from the side.

"Is she being ironic?" I asked my dad.

"Not at all," my mum said. "I love it when you plough into the side of other vehicles."

I grinned. "So do I," I said.

"Who wants candyfloss?" asked my dad.

His hand was up even before mine was.

We walked round for a bit. The funfair was still pretty crowded, though, and there was plenty to see but I was getting tired. Maybe it was a comedown from all the candyfloss and sweets and colas I'd been drinking, but suddenly everything started to look a little bit strange. There was music everywhere—from the carousel, from the stalls, from the bumper cars—and as it played, both sound and vision came in and out of focus.

I felt like I was underwater.

I felt like I was hovering above everyone.

I saw a woman with her little boy. They were holding hands and the little boy's face was lit up and excited, and the woman was smiling back. The boy turned to look at something and as he did so, it was like the woman's guard dropped. Her face was sad and her eyes were empty. Then the little boy turned round to say something and the woman smiled again, like she'd never been sad.

I saw a young couple, teenagers, by the shooting range. The girl fired a rifle at a target and hit it. She won a teddy bear and the stall holder gave it to her. But as he did so and she laughed, I saw her look at it like it reminded her of something, a different toy.

I saw a dad smile down at his son, then look up with a different expression on his face.

I saw a kid my age drop her ice cream on the ground and not even look at it as she walked past it.

I saw an entire carousel of people riding wooden horses, their faces equally expressionless.

And I saw my mum and dad, arms round each other, looking at the sights and listening to the sounds and it wasn't my imagination, my mum was crying.

I took her hand.

"Let's go home," I said.

We went home.

CHAPTER SEVEN

The days went on. From time to time I went to the park. I didn't cross the bridge, though. It wasn't like a conscious decision—*do not cross the bridge*—it was just something I didn't do anymore. Like when you're in a busy street with lots of traffic, you don't start walking in the middle of the road. There was a bridge, and I knew what was on the other side of it. I just didn't go there anymore. There were some things I was never going to do again.

Most of the time, though, things were all right. It was usually an OK time and what I liked about it best was that it was happening right now. I didn't have time to think about the past, or the things that had happened to me. I was living in the present and for a while that was a good place to be.

There were good things too. I got taller. I had birthdays. I got a new bike, a real one that wasn't a kid's bike. I discovered other books by the person who wrote *Chocky* (they were all pretty great, but *Chocky* was the best one as far as I was concerned).

And I made some friends. Two friends, to be precise. Their names were Ryan and Solange and they were my NBFs, my New Best Friends.

Ryan—name pronounced to rhyme with Brian—was a month younger than me, and it showed. He was excited all the time the way a puppy is excited all the time: always running around and making a lot of noise while not getting much done. If Ryan was a trading card, his strengths would include friendship, loyalty, and enthusiasm. His weaknesses would be short attention span, not being a genius and talking too much.

Solange—name pronounced how you imagine a French person would say "Solange"— was the total opposite of Ryan. She was a week older than me, but it felt like a thousand weeks. She was into science and books and wearing glasses in public: she was the smartest person in our school and her biggest disappointment in life so far was that she hadn't been "hot-housed" by her parents—whatever that means—and allowed to go to university when she was six years old (by way of contrast, Ryan's biggest disappointment was that his parents didn't let him eat a snail he once found in his lunchbox). Solange's strengths included intelligence, loyalty and being really good at finding ways out of a jam: her weaknesses were sarcasm, K-Pop bands and walking into walls while reading books.

We didn't go everywhere together, but we gave it our best shot. When I went to soccer practice, Solange and Ryan came along to watch, or at least to sit on the touchline eating crisps. When Solange went to her first chess tournament, Ryan and me went to all her matches and tried to coach her (even though Ryan didn't realise that all the pieces did different things to each other). And when Ryan broke his leg after he jumped off a wheelie bin trying to see if he could swim through air, Solange and me laughed and laughed. All right, we called the ambulance and rode with him to the hospital first. And then we laughed and laughed.

And one day, it was the last day of the summer term and the last day of the school year. I was sitting in my classroom with Solange and Ryan, and Mrs Mortonstone was addressing us.

"All right, everyone," she said, looking round the room, "Somehow, amazingly, it is your last day here, in this room, in this class, before you go up another year."

She sighed.

"It feels like I've been teaching you children for centuries. I mean that. Literally hundreds of years."

We looked up at her, faces of innocence. Even Ryan managed to look fairly innocent, which should have won him an Oscar, given that he was the one who managed to lose the school lizard (they found it a week later, unharmed and cheerful, in an amusement arcade inside the grabber machine, chewing on a stuffed rabbit)

"Anyway," she said. "Go peacefully amid the noise and haste and all that."

Solange put her hand up.

"Really?" said Mrs Mortonstone. "Now?"

"Put your hand down," Ryan whispered loudly. "We're about to be set free."

Solange didn't put her hand down. Instead she said:

"'Placidly', miss."

"I beg your pardon?" said Mrs Mortonstone.

"You said 'go peacefully amid the noise and haste'," said Solange. "It's 'go placidly'."

Mrs Mortonstone let out a sigh so deep I heard the windows vibrate.

"I'm going to miss you the most of all, Solange," she said.

"But I'm in your class for French next term," Solange said.

A reply was forming on Mrs Mortonstone's lips. Sadly it was drowned out by the bell.

"We're FREE!" Ryan roared, and punched the air as he leapt from his desk and ran to the door.

I walked home through the park with Solange and Ryan. Ali's ice cream van was nearby and it would have been rude not to pay it a visit.

Ali stood at his counter, massive arms bulging under his shirt. Not for the first time, I thought he was unusually large for an ice cream man, and wondered if somewhere there was a very skinny wrestler or bodybuilder who occasionally dreamed of selling Cornettos.

"Do we get a discount because it's the last day of school?" asked Ryan.

"No," said Ali in his very deep voice.

"Worth a try," said Ryan. "How about—"

"No," Ali said again.

Ryan looked annoyed.

"You don't even know what I was going to say," he said.

"True," said Ali, "But the answer's still no."

I showed Ali my money.

"Two strawberry cones with a flake and one pecan surprise with no flake," I told him.

"Can I—" Ryan began.

"No," I said.

We walked through the park with our ice creams.

"I wanted a flake," Ryan pouted.

"You are a flake," Solange replied.

"You pay, you choose," I told him.

Solange consumed her flake in one go, like a dragon.

"Another year over," she said. "I can't believe it."

"We're teenagers," said Ryan. "I'm not a kid anymore."

"The jury's still out on that," Solange said.

"What jury?" asked Ryan. Getting no answer, he picked up where he'd left off.

"I am so ready to be a teenager," he said, "I'm going to boss next year like—"

He thought for a moment. Then he thought for several moments.

"Like a—like a boss!" he finished.

Solange stopped licking her ice cream.

"You're going to boss it like a boss?" she said.

"Yeah!" Ryan shouted. He punched the air, and the top of his ice cream fell off. He picked it up off the ground and stuck it back in the cone. Solange and I exchanged revolted glances, but Ryan didn't care.

"I'll be the KING!" he shouted.

"The king," said Solange, in her driest voice.

"Yeah!" said Ryan, "The king of school."

"That's quite a goal," I said.

"Yeah," Solange agreed. "I mean, I thought I had big dreams. But I suppose becoming the world's first brain surgeon who's also a test pilot and a best-selling author is nothing compared to being... the King of School."

Realisation dawned on Ryan's face.

"Wait," he said. "Is this that—sarcasm thing I keep hearing about?"

Solange's face was a blank.

"Maybe," she said.

I corrected her.

"Maybe—*your majesty*," I said.

"Stop it!" said Ryan.

"Yeah, Louie," said Solange. "Leave Ryan alone. He's going to be the king of school."

Ryan beamed.

"Correct," he said. "I am."

That was the thing about Ryan. Other kids were sensitive or had easily hurt feelings, but Ryan had the hide of a rhinoceros when it came to rude remarks. His total obliviousness to personal comments was remarkable, and it drove Solange crazy (she once told me that on Sunday nights she stayed up late trying to think of stuff to say to him at school that would finally get to him and make him lose his temper. Needless to say, it never worked).

"I give up," said Solange.

She stopped. We had reached a bench. It was a normal-looking bench with a small plaque on it. The plaque read IN MEMORY OF LEN HE LIKED THE SEAGULLS.

"Here?" I asked her.

She nodded solemnly.

"This shall be the place," she said.

Ryan put his hands on our shoulders.

"Now shall we feast," he said.

The ritual complete, we sat down on the bench, opened our backpacks and took out our lunchboxes. We'd already had lunch at school, obviously, but as our parents were always putting stuff in our lunchboxes that we didn't like, we had developed a smart system for dealing with the unwanted fruit, vegetables and so forth. We traded them amongst ourselves.

Solange handed me her carrot sticks, and I gave her a mini-cheeseball in return.

"So, Louie," she said, "What are you looking forward to about next year at school?"

I thought about it.

"Does anyone like boiled eggs?" asked Ryan.

"Swap you for a mandarin," Solange replied.

I waited until the trade was over; then I said:

"I suppose the thing I'm most looking forward is the future finally happening."

"Wow," said Solange. "That's deep."

"Too deep for me," said Ryan. "You want that ham sandwich, Solange?"

"No, that's why I just took a bite out of it," Solange replied.

"Sarcasm?" asked Ryan. Solange nodded and he turned to me.

"The future?" he said. "What's so good about the future? The future is when we get older, and my dad said when you get older, you have to pay bills and work hard and be *responsible*. That doesn't sound like fun. That sounds like—"

Ryan thought for a moment, searching for the right words.

"—not fun," he finally said.

"The future's good because it's not the past," I said.

And I may have looked in the direction of the bridge.

Ryan rolled his eyes. Or at least he tried. He managed to roll one of them, like a chameleon having a panic attack.

"Not this again, Louie," he said. "You really need to get over it."

Solange hit Ryan on the arm, so hard that he actually fell off the bench.

"You can't just tell someone to 'get over it'," she told him as, wincing, he clambered back onto the bench. "And you know Louie had a hard time over—you know—"

"You can say her name," I told Solange. "I really don't mind."

I did mind, a lot, but I didn't want Solange and Ryan knowing that.

"Sorry," said Ryan, not looking particularly sorry for anyone but himself, "But I don't see the problem here. Louie was an imaginary friend. Just like the rest of us. And now he's not. Just like the rest of us. Big deal."

"Ryan," said Solange, and Ryan flinched. "I would so hate it if you were my imaginary friend."

"You know what," Ryan said. "I *hated* being an imaginary friend."

"What?" said Solange and I in unison.

"I hated it," said Ryan again. "Over there? In their world? It wasn't fun. It was cold. It rained. People were sad."

"That's what their world is like, dummy," Solange said.

"And that's why they need us," I said.

Ryan wasn't listening.

"You know what was the worst part?" he asked. "My kid."

Solange was looking at Ryan in disbelief.

"Your *kid*," she said. "What about your kid?"

Ryan spread his hands.

"We had nothing in common. I mean, *nothing*. He liked dancing. I mean, who likes dancing?"

"Millions of people like dancing," I told Ryan.

"Yeah," said Solange. "They make TV shows about it and everything."

"He hated sport," said Ryan.

"I hate sport," said Solange.

"Exactly," Ryan said.

"I expect he got enough exercise dancing," I said before they could bicker any further.

"Is that it?" Solange asked. "He liked dancing and he didn't like sport?"

"No," said Ryan, in the voice of someone saving their best card for last. He leaned over confidentially and said:

"His name was Bryan."

Solange threw her hands up.

"What's wrong with being called *Bryan*?" she asked.

"Really?" said Ryan. "You don't see it. Bryan, and—"

He pointed to himself.

"Ryan."

We stared at him blankly.

"*Ryan and Bryan*," said Ryan.

"It sounds nice," said Solange.

"Yeah, like you were meant to be friends," I said.

"I swear, sometimes I think you're doing it deliberately," said Ryan.

We sat there in silence for a while and Solange said:

"My kid was called Will. He was quiet and he liked drawing."

"Boring!" said Ryan.

"Shut up, Ryan," I told him. "Go on," I said to Solange.

"He used to draw these crazy pictures and make up stories to go with them. Dragons and spaceships and pirates and robots and knights in armour, all mixed up together."

She looked at the ground. An ant went by carrying a twig.

"He was going to be a writer, at least that's what he used to say. I hope he does. He had talent."

"Well, you'll never know," said Ryan. He picked up the twig and flicked it into the grass. "Because you're never going to see him again."

Solange was so shocked she forgot to punch Ryan in the arm.

"Ryan!" I said loudly. "That's not a good thing to say!"

"It's true, though," said Ryan. "My dad says that's just the way of the world."

I thought back to what my own dad had said:

"That's just the way things are."

Solange was angry now, and she might also have been crying a little.

"Your dad's a nincompoop!" she told Ryan.

Now Ryan was angry. Apparently you could insult him all you liked, but have a go at his family and that was something different.

"Take that back!" he shouted.

"Why?" asked Solange. "You don't even know what a nincompoop is."

Ryan thought for a moment.

"OK," he said. "Tell me what a nincompoop is and *then* take it back!"

Solange got up.

"You'll have to catch me first," she said.

"What?" Ryan asked, confused. "That doesn't even make sense!"

But Solange was off and running.

"See you later, Louie!" she shouted over her shoulder at me.

I sat there on my own for a while. Then I put my lunchbox in my backpack and headed off. The sun was setting over the bridge and it felt to me like the night was seeping in from the other side of the park.

I walked out of the park and down the road.

As I got nearer to the street my house was in, I had the strangest sensation that I was being followed.

I turned round.

Driving slowly down the road alongside me was Ali's ice cream van.

CHAPTER EIGHT

Ali pulled up beside me.

"Hi, Louie!" he called out in his enormous voice, and I swear some windows rattled in nearby houses. "You want an ice cream? On the house. It's my last scoop."

"No thanks," I said, "I already had one."

He nodded.

"Strawberry cone with a flake, I know."

Ali beamed.

"You want another one?"

I sat on the edge of the pavement, Ali beside me, and I ate the ice cream.

"That was delicious," I said.

"The last scoop's always the best," Ali said.

We stood up.

"Ali," I said, realising something. "Did you follow me home just to give me an ice cream?"

Ali looked uncomfortable.

"Maybe," he said.

"Why?" I asked. "I mean, don't get me wrong, I'm grateful but—"

"Because you looked like you needed it," said Ali. "And you've had a tough year."

I stared at him.

"What?" I asked. "How did you know?"

Ali spread his hands. They were very big hands: not for the first time, I wondered how he managed to scoop ice cream into the cones without crushing them.

"Louie," he said. "I'm parked in my van seven days a week, fifty-two weeks a year—"

"Wait," I said, "That's every single day of the year."

"What can I say? I love my job," Ali said.

"Don't you ever spend any time with your family? Or your friends?" I asked.

"One question at a time, please," said Ali, a little abruptly. I heard the sharpness in his tone.

"Sorry," I said. "Carry on."

"Thanks. I'm out here in my ice cream van every day. I have my casual customers and I have my regular customers. Mostly kids like you and your friends."

He smiled.

"Louie, I see a *lot* of kids. Happy kids, mostly, because who doesn't like buying an ice cream. But sometimes"—and here Ali turned towards me—"I see sad kids. And these last few weeks—no, months—you've definitely been a sad kid."

"I'm fine," I said.

"You're fine," Ali repeated. "Right, and ice cream is good for you. Louie, you're not fine. And I'm guessing it's because you found out."

"Found out what?"

"The same thing every other kid your age finds out. The imaginary friend thing."

I didn't say anything for quite a while. Then I asked:

"Really?"

Ali nodded.

"Yes, it's really that obvious."

"No," I said, "About ice cream not being good for you."

He laughed. Then he said:

"What was their name? Your friend?"

I sighed.

"Marcie," I replied. "She was great. She was smart, and funny, and she could get you with a Nerf gun when you least expected it."

Ali smiled.

"That's quite a testimonial," he said.

I wasn't sure what a testimonial was, but it sounded good, so I nodded.

"I wish I'd met her," Ali went on. "Not that I ever will," he said. Then he looked embarrassed. "Sorry," he said. "I didn't mean—"

"It's all right," I told him.

There was a silence, not unpleasant. Then I said:

"Ali, is it true?"

Ali looked a little bit nervous, the way grown-ups do when they're worried you're about to ask them something they don't want to answer.

"Is what true?" he asked.

"The whole friends thing," I said, and Ali relaxed. I think he thought I had been about to ask him where babies come from or something like that.

"My mum says everyone in the world—everyone in this world anyway—goes through the same experience."

Ali nodded.

"She's right. Everyone does. Every single person."

"Even—"

I stopped myself. Ali smiled.

"Yes, Louie. Every single person. Even Weird Ali the ice cream man."

"You're not weird," I said.

Ali raised a huge eyebrow.

"I mean, OK, you're out here all year round in all kinds of weather—I mean, I've seen you try and sell ice cream in a thunderstorm—"

"Have you ever eaten ice cream in a thunderstorm?" asked Ali. "It tastes *amazing*."

"No I haven't, and I'm not going to," I said.

"Why not?" asked Ali. "Scared your cone will be struck by lightning?"

Ali made a loud BZZZZIT! sound and laughed.

I didn't laugh.

"Ali, are you changing the subject?"

"No," said Ali. "Maybe. Sorry."

I let out a sigh. It was maybe a seven on a scale of one to ten.

"I tried to be like they wanted me to. I tried to be happy," I said. "Because, you know, it's a great life, here. The skies are always blue, the sun's shining all the time. It's like my dad says: there's no dark here."

"Except at night," said Ali.

"Except at night," I agreed.

"And in the basement with the lights off."

"Yes, in the basement with the—you get my point."

"I do," said Ali.

He looked serious now.

"Louie," he said, "in that world there's sadness and unhappiness and darkness. Here there's light and sunshine and smiles."

From where I was sitting I could see the side of Ali's ice cream van. There was a painting on the side, a happy family eating cones, their faces fixed in frozen grins. It reminded me of something.

"Ali," I said. "Don't you ever think the smiles are painted on? Because I see people here and they *look* happy, but there's something missing. And I know what it is."

"Louie, don't go down this path," said Ali. "It never goes anywhere good."

"I know why they're unhappy," I repeated. "It's because they all lost someone. Everybody lost someone."

I could hear my voice getting louder.

"And I think that's bad. I think it's wrong to live like that."

Ali said nothing for a long time. Then he said:

"You know the real reason people say I'm weird?"

"Because you sell ice creams during thunderstorms?" I asked.

"No," said Ali. "It's because I went back."

I stared at him.

"Go back?" I repeated.

Ali nodded.

"Over the bridge," he said.

"The—you mean *the* bridge?"

He smiled.

"There's only one bridge, Louie. And I went over it."

I couldn't take this in.

"But my dad said—my mum said—nobody goes back. *Nobody*."

Ali sighed. On a scale of one to ten, it was a ten.

"His name was Tom," he said.

PART TWO—ALI

CHAPTER NINE

I'll never forget the day I met Tom (Ali told me). I was four years old, and I was sitting under a tree, eating an ice cream. Even then I loved ice cream. I think I became an ice cream man just to get nearer to the stuff. I could have been a wrestler, but when I asked if the job involved ice cream, they laughed at me.

I'm rambling, aren't I? Sorry, I don't get to talk to people much outside of asking them what flavour they want and would they like a flake in it.

The day I met Tom I was sitting under a tree, eating an ice cream, and I was bored. The ice cream was nearly all gone and I had nothing else to do. I was counting the ants crawling up my leg when there was a thud and a football rolled up to my feet. I looked round to see where the ball had come from, but there was no-one. Then I heard someone shout, "Throw it back here!"

I looked up to see another kid, a boy my age. He was wearing glasses and a t-shirt with a picture of a parrot on it.

"Throw it back!" the boy shouted again.

I didn't throw the ball. For some reason, I kicked it. I felt my foot connect with the ball. It flew high in the air, bounced off a tree, nearly hit a baby buggy (I heard a woman's voice shout "Alan!" and I remember thinking even then that Alan was a weird name for a baby) and—to my total amazement—landed at the boy's feet.

The woman with the buggy went over to Tom.

"Watch where you're kicking that ball!" she shouted at him.

"It wasn't me," said Tom. "It was—"

He pointed at the tree where I'd been sitting, but I wasn't there.

"—him," Tim finished weakly.

The woman made a humphing noise.

"Come on, Alan," she said, and pushed the buggy off down the path.

Tom waited a few seconds, then went over to the tree and looked up into the branches.

"You can come out now," he said.

I fell out of the tree and landed on my bum.
Tom laughed. I laughed.

After that, we were friends. I don't have to tell you what it's like, Louie, because it's the same for all of us. We spent every possible minute of every single day together, and we just had fun. I don't think we ever argued, and if we did, we forgot about it straightaway. It was the best time of my life.

And if there were things that seemed a little odd, even at the time, well: I was a kid, and when you're a kid, lots of things seem odd. Life doesn't make much sense when you're a grown-up: when you're a child, it feels completely crazy almost all the time.

I remember one time me and Tom were playing in his garden. His mum—her name was Frankie—came out and she said:

"Tom, I'm making cold drinks, do you want one?"

Tom looked at me and I nodded.

"Lemonade, please," he said.

"Coming up," she replied.

"And the same for Ali," said Tom.

Frankie didn't say anything, she just laughed: and five minutes later, she brought the lemonade. One lemonade.

"I'm sorry," said Tom. "She always forgets to get two drinks."

It was true, but back then I didn't really think much of it. I think I just thought Tom's mum was a bit forgetful. And if Tom's parents acted like I wasn't there—well, so did my parents sometimes, it didn't mean they didn't like me. It was just one of those things. It happened, you forgot about it and life went on.

Then one day something happened that I couldn't forget about. I was playing football with Tom and a couple of other kids in the park. It was a complete mess: everyone was running round taking wild shots at the goal, and nobody was quite sure who was meant be *in* goal, and it was more like a riot than a game of football.

I remember I had a clear shot at the goal: the only problem was I didn't have the ball. Tom came up behind me with the ball.

"Pass it!" I shouted.

Tom didn't pass it. Instead, he aimed at the goal and kicked the ball as hard as he could—which wasn't hard enough. The ball rose through the air for a moment, then landed at the feet of the other team's goalkeeper.

"You should have passed it," I told Tom.

He shook his head, like there was something in his ear.

"Tom—" I began.

Just then another kid ran up to us. Her name was Sally and she was the only one of us who was actually good at football.

"Tom, you should have passed it," she said.

"That's what I said!" I shouted.

"Sorry," Tom said. "I got carried away."

"Never mind," said Sally. She smiled at Tom. "Are you coming to my party this weekend?"

"There's a party?" I asked.

Tom nodded. I waited for him to say, "Can I bring Ali?"

But he didn't.

He said, "Sure, I'll be there."

I stared at him.

"Tom?" I said.

"See you then," said Sally.

Tom didn't reply.

"Are you OK?" asked Sally.

"Yeah, Tom," I said. "Are you? Are you OK?"

"I'm fine," Tom said. "Just thought I heard—"

He smiled at Sally.

"See you on Saturday," he told her: and off he went.

After that—well, like I said, Louie, you know how it goes. I didn't see that boy again. I was pretty upset, but what can you do? Nothing, right. I went home to my mum and dad and told them what happened, and they hugged me a lot, and I cried, and I got on with my life. My life in this world, in our world. I made new friends—well, a few, one or two anyway—and I got a job. I bought the van, and I became an ice cream man. But I never stopped thinking about Tom.

Maybe I should have got a job where I didn't see kids every day. Maybe it would have been better if I wasn't outside the park all the time. Perhaps I should have got a job in a bank, or a cafe: but I'm not good with numbers and the only food I know about is ice cream. Besides, being in the van all day suited me. I could talk to people whenever I wanted to, and I could be alone whenever I wanted to as well. It's amazing how nice and peaceful an ice cream van with the shutters down can be.

I used to sit there, in the dark, with the cones and the wafers and the flakes and the sweet cold smell of ice cream all around me, and I would try and imagine what Tom was doing at that moment. Maybe he had gone to university, he was always smart, and now he was a lawyer or a doctor. I wondered if he was still living in the same town: perhaps he was travelling the world now on important business. Maybe he found someone, got married, and settled down. Maybe he never settled down. Maybe he was on his own, like me. I tried not to let myself have thoughts like that. Hopeful thoughts. Thoughts like that just led to disappointment. I knew Tom was never going to be part of my life again.

But.

Maybe.

Just maybe.

Maybe he was sitting at home, looking at a very old football, and wondering what I was doing right now.

I looked at my watch. It was seven o'clock in the morning. I had been sitting in the van all night. I got up from my seat, banged my head on the ceiling, said a bad word, and got out of the van. Then I ran to the park. I ran to the bridge. I ran *over* the bridge, to the other side.

For the first time in years, I was on the other side of the bridge.

It was cold. The sky was grey and full of clouds, which was probably why the park was so empty. But I didn't care. I had crossed the bridge and soon I would see Tom again.

I called his name a few times. Nothing. I was disappointed but then I thought, *what are you thinking, Ali? Tom doesn't live in the park, he's not a squirrel.* Even so, just to be sure, I ran around the park, shouting:

"Tom! Tom, it's me, Ali!"

Nobody replied and after a while my throat started to hurt. I sat down on a damp bench. I was beginning to wish I'd thought of a plan before I came out. The day was turning out to be a disaster. *Of course it is,* I thought bitterly, *I'm just an ice cream man.*

There were some people in the park, and as they passed the bench, they all stared at me. I soon realised why: in this world, where it was cold and grey, everyone was wearing raincoats and anoraks and warm coats. I was dressed in colourful shorts and a Hawaiian shirt with pictures of ice creams on. An old woman with a poodle passed my bench and as she did, said to the dog, "He'll catch his death if he's not careful."

It began to rain, which should have made me remember the times with Tom when we used to play outdoors in the rain until Frankie, his mum, told us to stop being stupid and come inside. But it didn't bring back happy memories: I just felt wet, and cold, and miserable.

A pigeon landed in front of me. It cooed at me.

"I haven't got anything for you," I said.

The pigeon gave me a bad look. I didn't blame it.

"This is hopeless," I said. "For all I know, Tom doesn't even live round here anymore. He could be on the other side of the—"

"Excuse me," said a voice.

A small boy was holding something out to me.

"You want some birdseed?" the boy asked. "To feed your pigeon?"

"He's not my—"

I stopped. There was something familiar about the boy. He looked like Tom. Then I realised: Tom would be my age now, a grown-up. He might even have kids of his own.

Kids of his own.

Before I could think this thought through, a hand came down on the boy's shoulder.

"Leave the gentleman alone," said a man's voice. "I'm sure if he wanted to feed the pigeons, he'd bring his own birdseed."

"That's right," I said. "But thank you for the kind offer."

"Not at all," said the man. He was tall and he wore glasses.

He looked at his watch.

"Come on, son, we've got to go," he said. "Nice meeting you."

I realised he was talking to me.

I looked up.

"Have a good day," I said.

But Tom and his son were already walking away.

How did I—

"Wait," I said.

I held my hand up and Ali stopped talking.

"They could see you? Tom could see you?" I asked. "I thought they couldn't see us anymore."

"I worked it out," Ali said. "They can see us if we're not important to them. We don't vanish if they don't care about us. We vanish when they *used* to care about us and they stop. That's because being a best friend is so intense, it's like you're a flame. One minute you're burning brightly and the next—"

He blew.

"Right," I said.

"You want me to go on?" Ali asked.

I nodded, and he continued:

How did I know it was Tom? After all, years had gone by and we were both no longer boys. But it was him. There was something about his face, the way he spoke—that, and the fact that the boy looked like Tom when he was a kid—I could be mistaken, but I wasn't.

Tom and his son were walking towards one of the exits that led to the big houses on the hill. I wondered why he was going that way when his mum and dad's house was the other way. Then I remembered that Tom was a grown-up now: he probably had his own home.

They were almost out of sight now. I looked at the pigeon, who was still looking for birdseed.

"What should I do?" I asked it.

It cooed in answer.

"You're right," I said. "I've come this far. It's too late to turn back now."

I got to my feet and walked toward the exit.

CHAPTER TEN

I almost ran out of the park. I was careful not to be seen by Tom and his son, but fortunately they were talking to each other and didn't notice me. I needed a plan, I realised. I couldn't just run up to them and shout, "Tom! It's me! Your imaginary friend!" I would wait until they'd gone inside, and a few minutes later, knock on the door and—

And what? Ask for directions? A glass of water? Say, "I don't suppose I could use your toilet"? All of these plans sounded creepy rather than useful. And besides, Tom had just seen me in the park, so if I went to his house, he'd know I was following him. Not for the first time, I wished I had a plan. It began to rain. There was a bus shelter just ahead of me, so I ran to it.

I watched as Tom, his son and the dog went into a large house: a few minutes later the boy came out, a school backpack over his shoulders, with a girl a little bit younger than him: I guessed she was his sister. They walked up the hill together.

A minute or two after that, a woman came out of the house, got into a very small car, and drove off. There was no sign of Tom. I wondered if he worked from home. I wondered if he had gone back to bed. Perhaps both.

Then Tom came out of the house, wearing a raincoat and carrying an umbrella and a briefcase. He walked down the road towards the bus shelter. Towards me.

I panicked. For some reason I didn't want him to see me. I reached into my coat pocket where I knew my hat was. It was my ice cream man's cap, but I didn't care. I crammed it onto my head and pulled it down over my eyes. I prayed Tom wouldn't notice me.

Tom didn't notice me. As he approached the bus shelter, the skies opened. It was raining cats and dogs.

The bus came. Tom stuck his hand out and it stopped.

Tom looked at me.

"Getting on?" he said.

I nodded and ran onto the bus after him.

The bus journey was pretty boring. The rain and the fogged-up windows meant I couldn't see out very well and what there was to see wasn't very interesting: boarded-up shops and cracked pavements and more bus shelters. I gave up looking out the window—which was when I saw Tom looking at me.

"Oh hello!" I said, because after all we had met, in the park.

"Hello," Tom replied cautiously.

"Me again!" I said, and even I could hear how weird I sounded, like a clown who'd lost his mind.

"Are you following me?" asked Tom.

"What?" I said. "No! No, not at all. Yes."

Tom raised an eyebrow. If he was scared of a strange person in wet clothes and an ice cream man's cap, he didn't say so. Instead he asked me:

"Why are you following me?"

I hesitated.

"First of all," I said. "You can see me, right?"

Tom's face was strange. Like he was worried but also like he was trying not to laugh.

"Yes, I can see you," he said. Then he said:

"Are you OK?"

When he said that I was so surprised and happy, I said:

"Oh yes. I'm fine, Tom. Thank you."

The moment I realised what I'd said, I put my hand over my mouth.

Now Tom did look worried.

"Do I know you?" he asked.

There was only one answer to that question: the truth. Well, some of the truth, anyway.

"Yes, you do," I said. "We used to be friends. A long time ago. A really long time ago. My name is Ali."

I smiled at Tom reassuringly. He didn't look very reassured.

"We used to play together in the park," I told him. "Remember?"

The bus stopped.

I could see from Tom's face that he didn't remember.

"I'm sorry," I said. "I should go."

I stood up and got off the bus.

I walked down the street. It was no longer raining but I felt cold and miserable. What had I been thinking? Years had passed since Tom last saw me. In that time he'd got older and had a family. It was me who'd stayed in the same place. I might drive an ice cream van, I realised, but in every other way I was a kid.

"A kid who never grew up," I said angrily to myself.

I took off my cap and squeezed the rain out of it. I was a failure, a wet failure. The only thing I could do now was turn round and—

Someone tapped me on the shoulder. I turned round.

It was Tom.

"There was a boy I used to play with," he said. "His name was Ali. It was a long time ago, but I remember. We played football and he came to my house and I remember my mother always forgot his—"

"She always forgot his lemonade!" I shouted.

Tom nodded.

"Ali?" he said.

"Tom!" I shouted and hugged him tight. Really tight.

Wincing, Tom removed my arms from his back.

"You got a grip there, Ali," he said.

"Sorry," I said.

Tom stepped back and looked at me. In my mind, I could see what he was looking at and I knew what he was seeing: a huge, weird, over-friendly guy in wet clothes holding an ice cream man's cap. I must have looked like I was down on my luck, or at least in need of a shower and a change of clothes.

I waited for Tom to fish out some coins so I could get a meal, but he didn't. Instead he said:

"Listen, Ali, my meeting doesn't start for an hour. Shall we go and get a coffee?"

I couldn't believe my ears. This was exactly what I wanted to happen.

"A coffee?" I asked. "You mean, like—a coffee?"

"Yes," said Tom, and he was smiling. "A coffee."

We were sitting in a coffee shop. It was still wet outside and everyone inside the coffee shop was steaming, but it was warm and dry so I didn't mind. Although I did keep looking round for the police, because I was sure Tom must have called them to come and take me away.

"Tom?" said a man. "Ali?"

I turned to see a man with a topknot and an apron holding a tray.

"A decaf latte," said the man, putting a coffee cup in front of Tom, "And a... coffee."

"That's me," I told him. "I got confused by all the names."

"No problem," said the man, and went away again.

I realised something.

"He can see me!" I told Tom in a loud whisper.

"Ali," said Tom. "I don't know how to put this but—everyone can see you."

He picked up his coffee.

"Right," I said. "Sorry. I've just had a long day. Week. Mmm! Coffee!"

I picked up my coffee and drank some.

"This is amazing!" I said.

"Wow," said Tom. "If you think a straightforward filter coffee is amazing, wait til you try a cappuccino. Or a mocha."

"I will!" I said.

Actually, I hadn't been talking about the coffee at all. What was actually amazing to me was the fact that, somehow, in this world, I seemed to be real. Tom could see me, the coffee man could see me—it was like I was part of their world.

But all those years ago, I had become invisible. As far as Tom was concerned, I didn't exist. And now here we were, talking and drinking coffee together.

Because he believes in me, I thought. Because he has no reason not to. Maybe it was because the first time he saw me today, I was talking to his son, to a kid. Even then he didn't know I was Ali. How could he? And now he knew who I was—his old, long-lost friend from when he was a kid—he still hadn't remembered that, as far as he was concerned, I was his *imaginary friend*.

Tom thought I was his childhood friend, his real childhood friend: and as long as he thought that, I *was* real.

I drank some more coffee. It really was very nice. Then I saw the clock on the wall.

"You probably need to get to your meeting," I said.

Tom looked at his phone.

"That's right," he said. "Let's walk out together."

We walked down the street.

"So, Ali," said Tom, and I can't tell you how great it was to hear him speak my name again, "Are you in town for long?"

"Maybe," I said. "I mean, I hope so. I mean, I don't really know."

I could hear myself starting to babble, so I stopped talking.

I could see Tom looking at me. Taking me in, as if for the first time.

I knew what he was seeing, too. A shabby figure with a silly cap, looking awkward and just… odd.

He seemed to be making a decision. I knew what it was: he was going to get out of here as fast he could and never see his weird old childhood pal again. I didn't blame him, frankly: he had a life and a family and a job where you had to carry a briefcase (and an umbrella) and I had nothing.

Then Tom said, "Come round. Tonight."

I stared at him.

"Really?" I said.

"Yes. Have dinner with us," said Tom. "Give me your number—"

"I don't have a phone," I said. I didn't need one: when you're an ice cream man, people generally come to you.

Tom's face changed. He looked a little sorry for me, and I realised he probably thought I was a drifter or some other kind of homeless person. He took out a pen and wrote an address on a coaster.

"Come to ours at eight," he said.

"I will!" I said, then: "Do I need to bring anything?"

"Just yourself," said Tom. He looked at his watch.

"I have to go," he said.

And he went.

I stood there for a few minutes, clutching the coaster. Then it started to rain again, so I put the coaster in my pocket before the ink ran.

Have dinner with us! Come to ours!

It was a dream come true. More than that, it was a miracle.

If you believe in miracles, that is. And right then, at that moment, I did.

CHAPTER ELEVEN

It was a long time until eight, pretty much the entire day. I could have walked back over the bridge and gone home for a few hours, but I was terrified that I wouldn't be able to return to Tom's world, so I went and sat in the park until night fell.

At just before eight o'clock I set off up the hill to Tom's house.

I rang the doorbell, and a boy answered. It was the same kid from the park.

"Hello again," I said.

"Hello," he replied. "You're Ali."

"Yes I am," I said.

"I'm Andy," said the boy and went back inside the house, leaving the front door open.

I went inside after him, closing the door behind me.

A woman appeared in the hallway. She was about my age, and she had a nice face.

"Tom?" she said. Then she saw me.

"You're not Tom," she said.

"No," I said. "I'm Tom's friend, Ali."

"That's right," she said. "Tom did say on the phone."

"Is he here?" I asked.

"No," she said. "He's late, but he shouldn't be long. I'm Sadie."

She smiled.

"Won't you come in?" she said.

I followed Sadie into the front room. Andy was sitting on the floor watching a cartoon with the girl who looked like him. On the sofa was a woman who looked familiar, if older.

Sadie said:

"Andy you've met. That's his sister Alison. And this is Tom's mum—"

"Frankie!" I said without thinking,

Frankie looked at me.

"I'm Ali," I said, "Tom's friend."

"Ali—" she said. "Sorry, doesn't ring a bell."

Sadie and Frankie gave each other a look. They probably thought I didn't see, but I did.

"Tom has so many friends," she said.

"I'm glad to hear it," I said.

There was a gap then, the kind that sounds like no-one can think of anything to say when really everyone has something to say but they don't want to say it.

Then I heard the front door open.

"Daddy!" shouted Andy and the little girl, and they ran out of the room. Sadie followed.

Frankie remained on the sofa. She narrowed her eyes and looked at me,

"I've got a very good memory," she said. "And I don't remember you."

Just then Tom came into the front room, followed by Sadie and the children.

"You made it, then," he said to me, then:

"Everyone, this is Ali, my friend from a very long time ago."

"We know!" shouted Alison.

Then Sadie said:

"Well?"

Tom looked puzzled.

"Well what?" he asked.

Andy hit him in the thigh.

"Mum wants to know did you get the contract?"

Tom looked at me.

"That's what my meeting was about. Getting the contract to supply—"

"Boring!" shouted Alison. "We just want to know if you got the contract!"

Tom said:

"I think so, yes."

Andy whooped.

Alison's face fell. Then she said to Sadie:

"Can we still give it to him?"

"I think so," Sadie said.

"Give what?" asked Tom.

In answer, Alison handed him a small paper bag. Tom uncrumpled it and took out a small, home-made thread bracelet.

"It's a consolation gift," said Andy. "In case you didn't get the contract."

"But we can still give it to you," Alison said. "Mum said."

"It's beautiful," said Tom. He slipped it onto his wrist.

"What a day of surprises!" said Sadie.

"I'll say," Frankie said.

We sat down to dinner. It was honestly the greatest dinner of all time. Not that I can remember a single thing we ate. I just had a brilliant time, being with Tom and his family. Sadie was really nice, and the kids were really funny, and Frankie—well, I knew she'd come round to me. People always do.

I helped clear up.

"That was such a great dinner," I told Sadie.

"Thank you," she said. "Just be grateful it wasn't Tom's turn to cook."

"Hey!" said Tom.

"Tom cooks?" I asked.

"In his own way," said Sadie.

Afterwards we went back into the front room and had coffee (I wondered if everyone in this world was mad on with coffee, or just Tom). The kids were sitting on the floor in front of me, and I was passing on some of my expert knowledge to them.

"The secret of selling ice creams is this," I told them. "Variety. You need to carry a lot of different flavours. But you also need the old stand-bys. I mean, yes, mochaccino is in right now, but that doesn't mean you can get rid of vanilla."

Andy nodded seriously.

"I wish I was an ice cream lady," said Alison, "I'd just eat it all."

"Now that," I told her, "is a rookie error."

Sadie stood up.

"Time for bed, kids," she said.

Tom stood up as well.

"I'll be back in a minute," he told me. "You and mum can have a chat."

Frankie and I sat there in silence. I had a feeling that either she didn't like me or, more likely, she *really* didn't like me.

She must have read my mind—or just seen me staring at her—because she looked me right in the eye and said:

"I just can't place you at all."

I said:

"It was a very long time ago. I used to come to your house and play with Tom."

"That hardly narrows it down," she replied.

Inspiration struck me.

"I remember one thing," I said. "I remember you'd come into the garden and you'd ask Tom if he wanted a drink, and he'd say he wanted a lemonade and so did I. And you always remembered his lemonade but you always forgot mine."

I smiled, to show it was a funny story. But Frankie wasn't smiling.

"Oh my goodness," she said. "Excuse me."

Then she left the room.

I sat there, looking at the fireplace. It was cold in the room and I wondered if anyone would mind if I put the fire on. I decided not to: it wasn't my house and besides, I didn't know how to.

Tom came into the room.

"Kids down?" I asked.

He nodded.

"They're such beautiful children," I said. "You're so lucky, Tom. You have a great family, a great house. Sadie's a wonderful person. I'm so pleased for you. You found happiness in this world. I'm glad I was able to see it."

Tom didn't say anything. I noticed he was looking at the floor.

"Tom?" I asked. "Is everything all right?"

Tom looked up.

"We need to have a talk," he said.

I was confused.

"A talk?" I said. "Tom, we've been talking all—"

Tom cut me off.

"Ali, do you remember when we were kids?"

I laughed.

"I certainly do!" I said. "We must have been in that park every day playing football. Wow! We were football crazy."

I leaned in.

"I was always taking shots that went wrong. Like the ball would bounce off someone's head, or their dog, or it would end up in the playground. And the funny thing was—"

I smiled at the memory.

"—you always used to get the blame."

Tom nodded.

"That's right," he said. "I always did get the blame."

I laughed again.

"One time I did a banana shot and I nearly knocked this girl off her bike."

"Yes," said Tom. He sounded far away, and I supposed he was just seeing the memory in his mind. "I remember, I got the blame."

"Yeah, that's what I said. I kicked the ball but you got the blame," I said.

"No," said Tom. "You're wrong. I was the one who kicked the ball."

"Tom," I said. "It was me. Every time."

"No," said Tom, "It was me. I remember now."

He sat up on the couch. He was looking at me, but he was also looking through me.

"I remember my mother saying to me, 'Tom, you've got to be more careful.' And I would say, 'Mum, it wasn't me, it was Ali'."

"That's right!" I told him. I could hear panic in my voice. "Because it was me!"

"But it couldn't have been Ali," said Tom.

"Yes it could!" I said loudly. "Because it was! Because I'm Ali!"

"You can't be," said Tom. "Because Ali wasn't real."

I was shouting now.

"No!" I yelled. "I'm real! I am! I'm your friend! Your best friend!"

Tom stood up. He opened the door. I could see Frankie and Sadie in the hall.

"Look," he said. "I don't know who you are—"

"I'm Ali!" I said. "Tom, I'm Ali!"

"—but if this is some kind of trick where you pretend to be my old friend so you can, I don't know, steal my identity or something, then you made a big mistake."

"I don't know what you're talking about!" I wailed.

"Because," said Tom, and his voice was cold now. "My old friend Ali isn't real. He never was. He only ever existed in a little kid's imagination."

I was crying now.

"Tom—" I began.

We were in the hallway now. Sadie put her arm round Tom.

Frankie opened the front door.

"Could you please leave," she said, "before I call the police."

Tom didn't look at me as I left the house.

I heard one of the children ask what was going on. Then the door slammed and I was on my own.

I walked through the park. The stars were the only light, and most of them were covered by clouds.

The bridge was in front of me. I didn't look back when I crossed it.

And that's the story of me and Tom.

PART THREE—LOUIE

CHAPTER TWELVE

Ali sat there on the kerb, looking more unhappy than anyone I had ever seen.

"And that's why everyone says I'm weird," he said. "Because I did it, Louie. I went back."

I tried to put my arm round Ali's shoulder, but his back was too big. It was like embracing a mountain.

"I don't think you're weird, Ali," I told him. "In fact, I think you're the bravest man in the world."

"What?" said Ali.

I took his hand. It felt as if I was holding a giant puppy.

"Ali," I said. "You went back over the bridge. Even though you didn't know what was going to happen. You risked getting hurt again, getting rejected. You're amazing."

Ali looked at me. His eyes were wet with tears but there was hope in them.

"You think so?" he asked.

"I do," I said.

I should have left it there, really.

Instead, I went on:

"You were amazing, Ali. If only you hadn't—"

I stopped. Some kind of brake in my brain had slammed itself on.

"If only I hadn't what?" asked Ali.

"Nothing!" I said. I sounded unconvincing even to me. I grinned, a big old fake old grin. "Let's leave it on 'You're amazing'."

"Let's not leave it there," said Ali. "So I'm amazing but also what?"

There was a new tone in his voice that I'd never heard before. I couldn't put my finger on it, but it certainly wasn't the voice he used to sell ice creams.

"Don't make me say it," I said.

"Why not?" Ali asked. "You can't leave me hanging. Besides, it can't be worse than anything I'm thinking. I mean"—and he looked me right in the eyes—"*can* it, Louie?"

I was trapped. I knew Ali wouldn't let it go. And he'd told me the truth about what had happened to him. Now he was asking me to be honest.

There was no way out of it.

"If only you hadn't—given up," I said.

Silence fell. And when I say "fell," I mean it fell like an iron gate.

Ali didn't speak anything for a long time.

Then he said:

"I was wrong. It *is* worse than anything I was thinking. Louie, I didn't give up. They threw me out. They said they'd call the police! They ran me out of town. I didn't have any choice apart from leaving—I mean," he went on, sounding more hurt than angry now, "what else could I have done? Stood there and shouted at Tom? Told him he was wrong and I was his imaginary friend? Because I could tell from the way he was looking at me that he already thought I was crazy— or worse, dangerous. I had to go, Louie, there was nothing else I could do."

Ali wasn't looking at me now. He was staring into space at something I couldn't see. I guessed he was remembering. Bad times or good, I couldn't say.

Then he said:

"That's just the way it is, Louie."

I stood up.

"Why does *everyone* keep saying that?" I said loudly.

"Because it's true," said Ali. "Because you can't change things. I know, I tried."

I was angry and frustrated. I knew deep down I should have apologised to Ali and gone home. But I had had enough. Had enough of the way we were all supposed to just lie down and take it. Like it was all our fault.

Something had to change, that was for sure.

"Did you, Ali?" I asked. "Because it seems to me you didn't really try."

Ali stood up. He really was the biggest ice cream man in the world.

"And what would you have done differently, Louie?" he said.

I was fired up now.

"All right," I said. "First of all, I would have told Tom the truth straight away. The moment I saw him in the park, I would have looked him in the eye and said, 'Tom, I know this sounds insane but remember your imaginary friend from when you were a kid? Well—here I am!'"

"He'd just say, 'Yes that sounds insane, because it is insane'" said Ali.

"Two!" I shouted. "I would be totally in his face. None of that 'I don't mind if you don't want to see me' stuff."

"You can't argue with someone who doesn't want to see you," Ali said. "And pretty soon he wouldn't be able to see me. I would have vanished away—"

I was on a roll now.

"And three!" I said. "I would have presented him with *evidence*. Stuff that would have proved you were who you said you were."

"Like what?" asked Ali. "Documents? Witness statements? Photographs? Louie, I was his imaginary friend. There's a clue in the name."

He put his hand on my shoulder.

"Louie," he said. "I know you're angry. And I get it. But when they don't believe in you, there's no point trying to change things."

I shook his hand off me.

"There's always a point," I said.

I walked off in the direction of my house. Behind me I could hear Ali's ice cream van starting off. For once the chimes were silent.

CHAPTER THIRTEEN

I opened the front door of my house and went inside. I must have still been angry, because as I went inside I heard the door slam behind me.

Mum and dad were in the kitchen, making dinner. At least my mum was making it and my dad was looking at cheese.

"Hi Louie," said my dad, putting down his cheddar, "how was school—"

I realised I didn't feel like talking, swerved out of the kitchen, and ran upstairs.

I heard my mum say, "At least you got as far as 'How was school?'. I never get further than 'Hi Louie' these days."

"Is this cheddar off?" my dad said in reply.

I ran into my room and closed the door behind me with a gentle slam. Then I sat down on the bed.

My room was no longer the crazed mess of toys, clothes, and kids' books that it had been when I was a kid. Now it was a crazed mess of games, clothes, and young adult books. There was a desk in there somewhere, which I could only find by following the power cable on my laptop.

But I wasn't going on my laptop right now. I had something more important to do.

I stood up and walked through a jungle of socks and underpants (why didn't my mum pick up all these dirty clothes, I wondered? Adults are so lazy sometimes) to the cupboard by the window. I took a deep breath, covered my face with one arm and opened the door.

And my childhood fell out. Party costumes (elves and superheroes), bows without arrows, swords without handles, board games without dice, remote controlled cars and tanks and drones without the remotes—all the stuff I promised my parents I'd take to the attic and all the stuff my parents swore they'd take to the charity shop. My past, in one cupboard. Like

Narnia, except there was nothing at the back of the wardrobe but old shoes and dead moths.

I stepped over a tin of mismatched Lego pieces and pulled out a cardboard box. Clearing some underpants off, I put the box down on the bed.

"LOUIE'S STUFF FOR CHARITY" my dad had written in his big, childish writing on the lid, perhaps in the belief that if you write "FOR CHARITY" on something, it will magically fly to the charity shop during the night. I took the lid off the box. On top there were some t-shirts I didn't care to look at right now (they had pictures of cute rabbits on and these days I was very much not into cute rabbits). I put the t-shirts to one side after a moment (they were *very* cute rabbits) and rummaged through the box.

There was a small, tattered pile of books. I reached in and pulled one out. It was my old copy of *Chocky*. There was a heap of little soft toys. Among them was Dog. I freed him from his companions and put him on the bed. Right at the bottom was my old Nerf gun. I took it out carefully. It was smaller than I remembered. But back then, I supposed, so was I.

There was a cluster of plastic bags at the back of the wardrobe. I put the toys and the book in it and slid the bag under the bed. Then I remembered something else: photos.

I opened my desk drawer, scrabbled through a pile of old keyrings, sparkly pens, and bird badges, and took out a small envelope. Inside it were some photos, the kind that you take with a camera where they develop instantly. I flicked through them. Me and mum, me and dad, me and mum and dad, me in a sandpit—

Me and Marcie.

"Hey Solange," Ryan said, "have you finished with that?"

"Ryaan," Solange replied wearily. "I literally just sat down. I haven't had time to start my lunch, let alone finish it."

"I know," said Ryan. "I just thought maybe you weren't hungry."

"Observe the tray," said Solange, "See the food. See the cutlery. It doesn't take a great brain to deduce that *I am about to eat my lunch*."

She slammed the tray down on the table.

Ryan gave me a grin and a *what's wrong with her?* look. Then he returned to staring at Solange's food.

"Stop looking at my lunch!" said Solange.

She turned to me.

"You know how some rich people have their own personal shopper?" she asked. "With Ryan, it's like having my own personal vulture. Hovering over my food every day, waiting for me to look away for a moment so he can—"

"Look up there!" shouted Ryan. "A big spider!"

He reached out a hand towards Solange's plate. She slapped it. Ryan winced and pouted.

"I can't help it if I'm hungry all the time," he said. "I think I have a tapeworm. In fact, I think my tapeworm has a tapeworm."

"Eat your lunch," said Solange. "Your own lunch."

We ate.

After a while (not a long while, he ate like a blizzard), Ryan stopped eating and said:

"Louie, you're very quiet today."

"It's called eating," said Solange. "Most of us don't eat and talk at the same time."

"I know," Ryan said, "But Louie hasn't said a word all morning. All day."

Solange put down her fork.

"Are you OK, Louie?" she asked.

"I'm fine," I said. "Just thinking."

I leaned over.

"Guys," I said.

"I hate being called *guys*," said Solange.

"Sorry," I said.

"I don't mind," said Ryan.

"Anyway," said Solange.

"Anyway," I said. "Um—*people*—I need your help."

Solange looked at me.

"What do you mean by *help*?" she asked. "Because I'm not doing your homework for you."

"Will you do mine?" Ryan asked, optimistically.

She ignored him.

"Louie?" she said. "You look really serious."

"He always looks like that," said Ryan. "I think it's trapped wind. We need to lie him down and massage his tummy with our fists."

I covered my stomach.

"It's not trapped wind," I said.

"Is it constipation?" asked Ryan.

"Ryan!" said Solange.

She turned to me.

"What is it?" she said.

I looked around to make sure no-one else was listening.

"I'm going back," I told them.

If I had expected more of a reaction, I didn't get one.

Ryan was busy looking at something on his finger that had probably come from inside his nose, and Solange just said, "Back where?"

"Yeah," said Ryan, "You need to be more specific."

"Back *there*," I said.

"That's not more specific," Ryan said.

Why were they so slow?

"Over there," I said, exasperated. "Over the *bridge*."

This time it sank in.

"THE BRIDGE!?" Ryan shouted. "Are you completely crazy—"

Solange punched his arm, hard.

"Are you completely crazy?" he repeated at a slightly less deafening volume.

Solange leaned forward, concern all over her face.

"Louie, you can't," she said. "There's no going back, you know that."

"Yeah!" Ryan said. "I heard one kid went over the bridge and he barely got to the other side before some ghosts ate him."

"Be quiet, Ryan," said Solange.

"It's true!" Ryan said. He paused. "Or maybe it was zombies. Either way, he went over the bridge and he got eaten. Ow!"

The last bit was because Solange had hit him on the arm again.

She looked around the room to see if anyone was listening in.

"Louie, what's going on?" she asked.

"Ali," I said.

"The ice cream man?" said Solange. She looked confused as well as concerned.

"Ali went back," I said. "Ali went back and he met his kid."

"Was his kid a ghost?" asked Ryan. "Or a zombie? I bet the kid was a zombie. That's probably why Ali's so weird. His zombie kid bit him and it affected his brain."

Solange raised her arm slightly. Ryan shut up immediately.

"Ali's—he's not the best person to talk to about stuff," she said.

"Yeah, he's weird," said Ryan. "That's why they call him Weird Ali."

"He's my friend," I replied. "And he's telling the truth. I believe him. He went back. He went over the bridge and he went back and he found his kid."

There was a long pause. Ryan covered his arm and said, gently (gently for Ryan, anyway):

"And how did that work out for him, Louie?"

"It didn't go well," I said. "But that's not the point—"

"It sort of is the point," said Ryan.

"Louie," said Solange, "What happened? With Ali and his kid?"

"He went about it the wrong way," I said.

"That's because there's no right way," said Solange. "It's all wrong way."

"The kid rejected him, didn't he?" said Ryan. "Imagine that. First Ali gets rejected when the kid can't see him anymore. Then he goes back and the kid rejects him again."

Ryan whistled sadly.

"I'd rather be eaten by a zombie," he said.

"Ryan's right," said Solange, "I mean, apart from the bit about the zombie. You can't go back. And the older you get, the worse it is."

"Yeah," Ryan said. "At least the first time round, you were a cute kid. Now you're an ugly old teenager, they're not even going to want to know you."

I looked at them with disappointment. It was the first time my two best friends had ever agreed about anything, and what they were agreeing about was that I was wrong.

"I don't care," I said to them. "I'm going."

I gave them my firmest look.

"And I need your help."

Solange sat back in her seat and laughed.

"You're kidding," she said. "We tell you it's the worst idea ever and you tell us you want our help."

"I don't *want* your help," I said, peeved. "I *need* your help."

"Nice," said Ryan. "You've totally won me round."

He grinned.

"See? I can do sarcasm too."

"I'm sorry," I said. "But please, you're the only ones who can help me."

Ryan and Solange looked at each other.

"No," said Solange.

"No way," said Ryan.

"Why not?" I asked. I sounded desperate.

"Because you'll just end up getting hurt," said Solange.

"Yeah, and hurting you is my job," Ryan said.

"Because it's dangerous out there," Solange said.

"Which is why I need your help," I said.

"And because we're your friends," said Ryan.

"But that's it," I told them. "If you're my friends—which I know you are—then you'll help me. Even if it's stupid, and doomed, and dangerous, you'll help me. Because that's what friends do."

Ryan looked at Solange.

"He did it," he said. "He played the friend card."

Solange nodded. Then she turned to me.

"OK," she said. "What do you need?"

CHAPTER FOURTEEN

It was late and the moon was out. The path through the park was silver in the moonlight as I walked towards the bridge. Solange and Ryan were already there.

"Rats, he's here," said Ryan on seeing me approach.

"Yeah," said Solange, "We were hoping you'd changed your mind."

"Thanks," I said. "You won't regret this."

"Of course we will," Solange replied. "It's a terrible idea and it's going to end in disaster."

"Even if there aren't any zombies," Ryan added.

I got down to business.

"Solange, I told your parents I'm staying over at yours tonight."

Ryan looked hurt.

"Why couldn't you tell them you were staying over at mine?"

Solange gave him a look.

"Nobody stays over at yours, Ryan," she said.

Ryan nodded, then frowned.

"Why is that?" he asked.

"We might if you ever wash your socks," Solange replied.

"So if your parents call my house," she said to me, "I'll pick up first and tell them you're asleep."

Ryan laughed.

"I can't believe your parents still have a land line," he said.

"And I can't believe *your* parents didn't get a puppy instead of you," Solange said.

She turned to me again.

"Louie, what if you're gone more than one night?" she asked. "What do we do then?"

"I know!" said Ryan. "We put a dummy in Louie's bed so it looks like he's sleeping."

"I'll be back by then," I told Solange. "I'm just going to find Marcie, prove to her that I am who I say I am and when she realises that I'm her oldest and best friend ever—"

"—if she realises—" said Ryan.

"Then I'll take it from there," I finished.

Solange looked doubtful.

"I'll be fine," I said. And I nearly meant it.

"I know you will," said Ryan. "Because of—"

He took off his backpack.

"—because of—" he went on, trying to open the bag.

"—because—"

The bag wouldn't open. Solange and I looked on confused as Ryan wrestled with the straps.

"Oh, give it to me," Solange said. She took the bag and opened it with one movement of her hands. Then she looked inside.

"What the—" she began.

"Give me that!" said Ryan. He took the bag back, reached inside and pulled out a coil of rope and something round. Something large and round and heavy-looking.

"No," said Solange.

"Yes," said Ryan.

It was an old-fashioned diving helmet, the kind that's made from brass and has little circular glass windows.

"What's that for?" I asked.

"I saw it in a movie," Ryan said. "You tie one end of the rope round your waist"—he demonstrated—"and the other end round a tree. Then you put on the helmet—"

Before I could protest, he jammed the heavy metal helmet onto my head.

"I can't breathe!" I yelled.

"No problem," Ryan said. "You just need to attach it to a supply of air."

Solange gave him her most cutting look.

"And do you *have* a supply of air?" she asked.

"Really suffocating a lot now!" I said in a muffled voice.

Ryan looked sheepish.

"No," he admitted.

"Get it off him," said Solange.

Together they managed to wrestle the helmet from off my head. I gasped and gulped and staggered around for a bit.

"Sorry," said Ryan.

"No problem," I told him and began untying the rope.

"You need that so we can pull you back in!" protested Ryan.

"I'm going to the other side of the park, not the Moon," I reminded him.

"You know this is a terrible plan, right?" said Solange.

"Yeah," said Ryan. "What if she doesn't believe you? What if she moved house?"

I smiled.

"I'll cross that bridge when I come to it," I said.

Solange rolled her eyes. Ryan grinned.

"Like literally!" he said. "Because you are *literally* about to cross a— ow!"

"Sorry," said Solange. "Habit." Then:

"Good luck, Louie."

"What she said," said Ryan.

"Don't worry," I told them. "It's going to work."

"Take the helmet," he said. "Just in case."

I opened my arms.

"No!" said Ryan. "No group hugs!"

Solange pushed him towards me. Then she hugged us both.

I stepped back.

"See you on the other side."

Ryan was about to speak.

"Not literally," I told him.

I waved at them both, and walked towards the bridge.

The moon lit my way and I could see everything clearly: the stream below the bridge, glinting in the moonlight, the pictures that people had stuck to the bridge, and the path in front of it.

I was over the bridge now, and in what I still called Marcie's side of the park. Even though it was a moonlit night on both sides of the bridge, it felt colder on this side, and darker too. There were clouds in the sky, obscuring the moon and the stars, and everywhere I could see big dark shadows. I looked back to where I'd come from. Was it my imagination or did the other side of the bridge—my side—still have the faint glow of evening?

Then the sound of a police car's siren made me jump. I zipped up my coat and pulled the hood over my head and began to walk through the park.

In some ways, the park was how I remembered it from when I was a kid, but in other ways—it wasn't. For a start, it was a mess. There was litter everywhere: on the grass, on the paths, and in large heaps around the litter bins, which were overflowing with rubbish. Glass glinted in the moonlit and I could see the occasional rat scurrying in to take a bit of food back to its den. Benches were smashed and broken, flowerbeds were trampled, and trees had their branches snapped off. Instead of ducks, the ornamental lake was full of shopping trolleys and even traffic cones.

The playground was still there, though, even if the gate was lying on the ground, broken. I stepped over it and went inside. The climbing frame was on its side, like the busted skeleton of some alien creature. The slide was dented and overgrown with weeds, and the swings where Marcie and I used to spend hours flying up into the air were gone, just lengths of chain dangling in the air. Even the bouncy elephants were out of action, their springs busted and gone.

I looked around the playground, trying to remember how it had been, how I and Marcie would—

WHOOSH!

A tiny object dived out of the night straight at me. I ducked and it chirruped as it circled my head. It was a bat.

I don't remember bats, I thought. I watched as it joined its friends high in the trees. *Bats are fine*, I reminded myself, and left the playground. I wasn't scared of bats. I liked bats.

Something howled and I nearly jumped out of my skin.

"That was a dog," I said out loud to myself. "Just a dog."

But I walked a little faster.

I'm fine, I told myself. *This is the same old park you used to know, just a little bit rundown, that's all. Well, a lot rundown, but it's OK. And it's not far from here to Marcie's house, she'll be there, and everything will be—*

"Wake up, kid!" said a voice.

I looked up. I was about half a centimetre away from walking into someone. Three older kids, skinny and wearing black (*just to make it easier to walk into them*, I thought).

"Is he all right?" asked one of the boys. He had a quiet, grating voice that didn't seem to know if it was high or low.

"Let's ask him," said the first boy. His voice was surprisingly deep. "Are you all right?" he said.

"Honestly?" I said. "I'm a bit lost."

I was, too. Maybe it was because the park had changed since I was last here however many years ago, or just because it was dark, but I wasn't sure which way the exit to Marcie's street was.

The first boy nodded.

"Easily done," he said. "But you really shouldn't be here."

"Yeah," said the third boy, who had a very nasal voice, "It's not safe in the park at night."

"That's right," the first boy said. "There's a lot of bad people around."

They laughed at this and I joined in.

"I can believe it," I said. "Listen, I'm looking for someone. Do you know—"

I realised the three boys had surrounded me. They began to circle me.

"Looking for someone?" asked the first boy.

"We're all looking for someone," said the second boy.

"Or *something*," the third boy said.

I had no idea what they were talking about, but I was starting to feel uncomfortable.

"Right now," the third boy continued, "I'm looking for a new backpack."

"A new backpack?" I repeated, stupidly.

"Yeah," said the boy. He really did have a very nasal voice. Everything he said sounded like a wasp in a jar.

"A backpack like yours. Just like yours," he said, then:

"Ah, what the heck. I'll just take yours."

And before I could run, the other two boys grabbed me and pinned my arms so I couldn't move. The boy with the nasal voice took something from his pocket.

It was a knife.

"No!" I shouted.

"Shut up!" the boy said.

He reached out with the knife and cut the straps of my backpack. Then he pulled the bag off my back. I watched in horror as he emptied the contents of the backpack onto the ground.

"Stop it!" I yelled.

The boy ignored me. He was looking at my stuff on the path. My old copy of *Chocky*. My Nerf gun. A wallet of photos. And Dog.

"What is all this?" he said. He picked up the Nerf gun and aimed it at the others.

"Look out!" said the boy with the deep voice. "He's got a gun!"

They all laughed. The second boy leaned down and picked up Dog.

"Leave that alone!" I said.

The second boy waggled Dog's head.

"Leave me alone," he mimicked. "It's not my fault I'm a loser."

He dropped Dog on the ground.

"This is all kid stuff," he said.

"Maybe he's got money," said the boy with the nasal voice.

"Yeah, let's roll him," the second boy said.

I didn't know what that meant, but I could guess.

I took a step back—and tripped over a sack of rubbish.

They began to close in on me.

I heard a roar.

I looked up.

Something was charging towards us.

Something big.

Something roaring.

CHAPTER FIFTEEN

It was a man beast. Hairy, fierce and furious.

"RRRRAAAAARRGGGGHHH!" it roared.

"Run!" shouted the boy with the nasal voice, nasally.

The boys ran.

I was too scared to move, and besides, I was lying on the ground.

The man beast crouched down next to me. It sniffed me, then it bared its yellow, broken teeth. I closed my eyes.

"Please don't eat me!" I said. "I didn't do anything wrong!"

The man beast looked at me and I swear I could see intelligence in its eyes.

"Eat me?" it said. "I'm hungry, son, but I'm not that hungry."

It stuck out a filthy hand.

"Come on, get up," said the man beast.

I took his hand and he pulled me to my feet.

"That's better," he said, then:

"My name's Jones. And you?"

"I'm Louie," I said.

"And is this all your stuff?" Jones asked.

I nodded. Jones knelt down and put everything back in the backpack. He tied a knot in the broken strap and gave it back to me.

"Thanks," I said.

"Next time don't go wandering around on your own in the dark," said Jones.

He looked at me.

"You're a bit young to be out in the park at this hour, aren't you, Louie?"

"Maybe," I said. I was feeling a lot better now. "But the last time I was here, this place was a lot different."

"That must have been a *long* time ago," said Jones. "This whole town is getting worse. It used to be a nice place to live, but—I don't know—it's like everything's getting darker."

"My dad says this world can be a dark place," I told him.

Jones nodded.

"Your dad is correct," he said. "Which begs the question—what are you doing here on your own?"

I sighed.

"It's a long story," I said.

Jones nodded.

"They usually are," he said. "But tell me later. We need to get to a safer part of the park."

He strode off. I followed.

If I'd thought about it for more than two seconds, I might have questioned the wisdom of following a man beast through a dark and dangerous park at night. I mean, I could see now that Jones wasn't actually a beast, just a man with a very long and messy beard (I swear there were twigs in it) and a coat which must have been nice about two hundred years ago, but he was still pretty terrifying and for all I knew he was taking me back to his lair to eat me.

"Where are we going exactly?" I asked.

"Somewhere better," Jones replied.

And he licked his lips.

At that exact moment I saw car headlights. We must be near a road, I thought, which meant that wherever we were going, we were near the park exit. If things went wrong, I could always make a break for it.

The path in front of us widened. One of the park lamps was still working, and it cast a yellow glow ahead. I could see a large grassy area.

There were people on the grass. I couldn't see what they looked like, but there was a small crowd of them.

Jones saw me hesitate.

"This way, kid," he said. "Come on."

"What's going on?" I asked. I sounded nervous.

"Relax," he said.

"No," I said. "I want to know what's happening here. Who are those people?"

"Friends," said Jones. "My friends, anyway."

I didn't know what to do. On the one hand, Jones had rescued me from the boys. On the other, he might be leading me to a worse fate. It was hard to tell.

As we got nearer to the crowd, I smelt something.

"What's that smell?" I asked.

"Soup," said Jones. "Made from the bones of boys."

"What?" I said.

"I'm kidding," Jones said. He sniffed the air.

"I think it's minestrone tonight," he said. "Hey Pete!" he called out.

One of the figures in front of us turned round. He was a big man in an old Army jacket.

"Jones?" he said. "Is that you?"

Jones walked up to Pete and shook his hand. Then Pete saw me.

"Who's this?" he asked.

"My dinner," said Jones.

Pete considered this.

"Not much meat on this one," he said.

"Maybe I'll just have the soup, then," said Jones.

I stuck my hand out towards Pete.

"My name's Louie," I said.

"Nice to meet you, Louie," said Pete. "Are you hungry?"

"Now that you mention it, I'm starving," I said.

Pete smiled.

"Come with me," he said.

"What's this called?" I asked Jones.

We were sitting around a small fire. Pete was opposite us, doing some serious damage to a bowl of soup, and Jones was blowing on a cup of hot tea.

"Vegetable thali," Jones replied. "With naan bread and rice."

"It's incredible," I said. "Do you have this every night?"

"Not every night," said Jones, and I wondered what his life was like and how he'd come to be someone who queues up for food at night in a park.

Then a snaggle-toothed grin broke out on his face.

"Hey," he said, "You never finished telling me your life story."

I gave him a look.

"I don't think I *started* telling you my life story," I said. "In fact, I didn't tell you anything about myself other than my name."

"I know you're called Louie," Jones said.

"You don't," Pete chimed in. "Names change around here," he told me.

"And I know you're looking for someone."

I stared at him.

"How did you know that?"

"Well," said Jones. "You're not on the run because nobody, not even a kid, goes on the run with nothing but a Nerf gun and a toy dog. So—"

He took a swig of tea.

"—you must be looking for someone."

"Nice work, detective," said Pete. Then he looked at me and said: "Welcome to the club."

"What?" I asked. "What club?"

"See, the thing that Jones isn't telling you," said Pete, "is that *everyone* here is looking for someone."

He waved a hand at all the people sitting by the fire.

"Everyone?" I asked.

"Everyone," said Pete.

Jones nodded.

"Louie, everyone here has lost someone. A partner, a loved one—a friend."

"Even you?" I asked Pete. Pete nodded. He was still smiling, but his eyes told a different story.

"And you?" I said to Jones.

"Yeah," said Jones. "And I was like you. I went out and tried to find them. I looked all over, everywhere I could think of. I looked and I looked, until one day I couldn't look any more," said Jones. "And while I was searching for what I'd lost, I lost what I had."

Jones looked down and touched his wrist. I saw that instead of a watch, he was wearing a bracelet made of thread.

Pete patted his back.

"Same for all of us," Pete said.

"Well," I said. "That's not going to happen to me."

Jones looked up.

"You sound pretty sure of yourself," he remarked.

"Oh, I am," I said.

"Don't tell me," said Pete. "You've got a plan."

"I do!" I said.

"Always good to have a plan," Pete said. Then:

"Let me guess. You've got, what, evidence. Things that'll trigger memories. Good memories."

I stared at him.

"How do you know?" I asked.

"Oh, Pete's got great intuition," said Jones. "He's very intuitive."

There was something in his voice—not unpleasant, just slightly mocking—that made me flare up with anger.

"Yes, I do have a plan," I said. "And it's a good one. I'm not just going to rush up to them when I find them and yell in their face and shout—"

"Hi Marcie!" said Pete.

I was speechless. My face must have been registering a hundred emotions—a thousand. Disbelief, shock, amazement.

"What did you just say?" I asked.

But Pete was no longer sitting down. Nor was Jones. They had both scrambled to their feet.

A girl was standing there. She was wearing warm clothes and she was carrying mugs of tea.

She was older, but I knew exactly who she was right away.

"I didn't expect to see you here on a school night," Pete was saying to her.

"I couldn't keep away from you guys," said Marcie.

"Knew it," said Jones.

"And," Marcie said. "Mum fell asleep on the sofa so I thought I'd come out on the food run tonight and see if I could help out."

"Well, it's good to see you anyway," said Pete.

"You too," said Marcie. "Anyone for tea?!" she shouted, and walked on.

I couldn't move. I was welded to the spot. I was like a statue, only less mobile. Frozen to the spot? That was me.

I think you get the idea.

I had been waiting—how many years? I couldn't say, my mind was emptier than a swimming pool with a shark in it—waiting for so long for this moment, and now it was here, now it was actually happening, I couldn't do anything.

Jones and Pete turned to see me standing there. There must have been something about my stunned, paralysed, struck-dumb face that concerned them.

"Are you all right, kid?" Jones asked.

"It's her," I finally managed to say from out of the side of my mouth, "It's Marcie."

Pete looked at me, puzzled.

"Yeah, we know it's Marcie," he said. "She comes here most nights."

"No," I said, "It's *Marcie*. It's *her*."

"What do you mean?" said Jones.

Pete nudged him.

"His Marcie," he said.

Realisation crept across Jones' face like dawn over the ocean.

"Ohhhhh," he said.

"Is she, Louie?" asked Pete. "Is she your Marcie?" he asked.

"Yes, she's my Marcie," I said. I could hardly say the words. It felt like there was an egg in my throat.

Jones and Pete exchanged a look.

"OK, Louie," said Jones. "Listen to us. You need to be calm."

"That's right," Pete said. "Take it easy, one step at a time. Find a moment to speak to her."

"It's like you said," Jones said. "Don't just run up to her and shout—"

But I was gone.

She was standing at a trestle table that was covered in soup bowls and plate. There were two plastic basins in front of her. One was red and one was blue. Marcie was washing plates in the red bowl and rinsing them in the blue bowl.

She saw me staring at her. I didn't shout. I didn't yell her name. I didn't throw my arms around her and crush her in a powerful hug. I just said, in a quiet, normal voice:

"Hello, Marcie."

Marcie looked up from a plate she was scraping.

"Hello," she said, then:

"Sorry, do we know each other?"

I'll admit I was hoping she was going to say, "Louie! Is that you?" or maybe even shout it and leap over the table and envelop me in a powerful hug. I would have been happy with a double take—where she looked at me, said, "Oh hi, Louie" in a casual way, then realisation dawned and she yelled out my name, leapt over the table and so on. So yes, it was a disappointment when she did none of those things.

But I had prepared for this moment. Ali's experience with Tom, while horrible, had at least warned me what to expect. Neither a warm welcome nor cold indifference: just the experience of meeting someone again—someone you really care about—who has no memory of you whatsoever.

I had expected Marcie's reaction and I was ready for it.

I reached into my backpack. The first thing I pulled out was *Chocky*, which wasn't quite what I had in mind. But it was a start.

"Look!" I said.

Marcie peered at the cover of the book.

"Lovely," she said. "Did you write it? Am I supposed to remember you from a book? I'm sorry, I—"

I reached into the backpack again and this time I took out Dog.

"Dog!" I said, and I may have said it loudly. "Dog!"

A strange look came over Marcie's face. She was smiling, but also she seemed wary.

"Yes," she said, a fixed smile on her face, "You're right. It *is* a dog. Bow wow!"

"No!" I said. "I mean—wait. Please!"

Marcie must have heard the urgency in my voice, because now she looked concerned.

"Thank you!" I yelled. I reached in the backpack again. My hand brushed the Nerf gun. For a second I thought of pulling it out and shooting a Nerf ball at her. A picture came into my mind—me in the back of a police van.

Then my fingers found what I'd been looking for all along.

I took out the wallet of photos.

"Look," I said.

I gave her the photos and watched as she looked at them. They were all pictures of me and Marcie—in the park, in the playground, on the swings. Evidence that would prove to anyone that we were friends.

"Um," said Marcie. "These are very nice but—why are you showing them to me?"

"What?" I said. "Because—look—"

I took them back and my jaw dropped.

They were all pictures of me on my own. Me on the roundabout, me on a bench, me with the Nerf gun. Marcie wasn't in any of them.

"I don't understand," I said. "Marcie, I don't get it."

Marcie didn't say anything. She looked very uncomfortable and I couldn't blame her. Some weirdo appears out of nowhere, says he knows her and shows her a selection of completely random stuff? If I was her, I'd be looking round for help.

"You OK, Marcie?" a voice said. I looked up to see a big man in a duffel coat standing by Jones and Pete with a big, heavy frown on his face.

"Yes, fine," said Marcie, but the tone of her voice said no, she wasn't OK.

"He's just a little over-excited," said Jones to the man. "Too much vegetable thali. We'll take care of him, Mister Atta."

The man nodded.

"See that you do, Tom," he said.

I felt my eyes widen.

"Tom?" I said. "You're Tom?"

Mister Atta was still speaking.

"This boy scared the hell out of Marcie," he told Jones.

"He didn't!" said Marcie. "And I told you, I'm fine."

Mister Atta, who was clearly the boss, looked down on her.

"Maybe you should go home, Marcie."

"Honestly, everything's OK," said Marcie. "I just feel a little bit… discombobulated."

Marcie looked confused, and I could see her thinking: where did *that* word come from?

"You did really well tonight," said Mister Atta, and even I could hear the missing word in that sentence: *considering*.

Marcie looked furious. She was furious. She took off her apron and threw it at the ground.

Then she turned to me.

"Thanks a lot, whoever you are," she said.

I made one last attempt.

"It's me!" I said. "It's Louie!"

She shook her head.

"Leave me alone," she said. "I don't know any Louie."

I watched as she stormed off out of the park.

They were packing up the soup kitchen. Tables were folded and pots were stacked and loaded into the back of a van.

Jones—or Tom—and me sat on a bench watching the sun come up.

"I tell myself I wouldn't have the sunrise if I still had a home," said Tom.

"Does it help?" I asked him.

"Until the sun comes up," he said. "Then it's just another day."

"Was it because of Ali?" I said.

"In a way," said Tom. "After he went, I kept thinking about what he'd said. I knew he couldn't be my imaginary friend from when I was a little kid, because how was that possible? Imaginary friends aren't real."

"We're real all right," I said. "And how would you like it if someone you cared about didn't believe in you anymore and you just—disappeared—from their lives?"

"I wouldn't like it at all," said Tom. Then he said:

"Louie, you've got to let her go."

"No way," I said. "I've come this far, Tom, and I'm not giving up. Ali gave up and look what happened to him. He's sad and he's alone and—"

"I didn't mean give up for your sake," said Tom. "I meant for Marcie's."

He fingered the thread bracelet.

"I'm sorry about Ali," he said. "He has a life, though, and a home. If he wanted to, he could find someone and make a fresh start. But me—I lost everything. Ali came back and made me remember, and once you remember, you can't forget. You obsess to the point of letting everything else go. Do you want that to happen to Marcie?"

"Maybe I do," I said. "After what she did to me—after what all you people did to us—maybe she should suffer. Feel some of the pain we feel. Because I did everything I could to get back with her. Because that's what friends do. Real friends."

"Louie—" Tom began. He looked as sad as any human being could look.

"If Marcie doesn't believe in me," I said, "then I don't believe in her."

I walked away from him.

I kept walking until I was right at my own front door. I opened it and went in. I could hear my parents' voices. My mum was on the phone to someone.

"He's not at Ryan's and he's not at Solange's—" she was saying to someone.

Then she saw me.

"I'll call you back," she told the other person and let the phone fall to the floor.

She threw her arms round me.

"What's all this noise?" I heard my dad say. "Did you drop something—LOUIE!"

My dad ran down the stairs. He joined in the embrace.

"You're breaking my ribs!" I said.

My mum stood back.

"Where have you been?" she asked.

"I'm sorry," I said.

My dad said:

"Answer your mother, Louie. She's had a terrible night because of you. And," he added, "so have I."

"You lied to us," said my mum. "You said you were with your friends and you weren't."

"What happened?" my dad asked. "And this time, don't lie."

I looked at the floor and said nothing. Then I decided they deserved better. I lifted my head up and, ashamed, said:

"I went looking for Marcie."

"Oh, Louie," said my mum.

"Aren't you too old for—" my dad began.

My mum touched his arm and he stopped talking.

"It's over," I told them. "I won't be going back. I'm sorry."

And this time I hugged them.

PART FOUR—MARCIE

CHAPTER SIXTEEN

I didn't run out of the park. I didn't want everyone thinking I was some stupid girl who couldn't cope at the soup kitchen and got freaked out by some little weirdo and ran away crying to her mummy.

I walked out of the park instead. I may have walked quickly, true, and when I was out of sight of everyone I may have sat at a bus shelter for a few minutes to let my head clear. After all, I had just had a pretty strange experience. Not staying up all night in a park with some homeless people—I'd been working at the soup kitchen for months and I was pretty used to the job—but that boy.

I tried to remember what he'd said and done, and all the business with the backpack and the toys. He seemed like a nice enough kid, if a bit over-friendly—a *lot* over-friendly. And he was totally peculiar, showing me his crumpled old book and his toy dog—and what was up with those photos? The same grinning kid posing on his own all over the park.

I shivered a little. The boy—Louie, he said his name was—had really freaked me out. I felt completely—

Discombobulated.

I got up and walked back home to the flat. At the sound of my key in the lock, my mum called out from the kitchen:

"I'm making breakfast!"

"Not hungry!" I shouted back, and went to my room.

A few minutes later, there was a knock on the door.

"Can I come in?" I heard my mum say.

"Sure," I said, "Why not?"

The door opened.

"Thanks," said my mum.

She came and sat on the bed next to me. I pulled my legs up closer in case she was planning to do anything unexpected, like hug me or smother me in kisses. I was not a smother me in kisses kind of person.

Mum looked at me hunched up on the bed.

"Tough night?" she asked.

"It was all right," I said.

"Is that why you came up the stairs like a rocket?"

"OK," I said. "It was mostly all right."

My mum was silent for a moment, which I knew wouldn't last. Then she said:

"I don't like to say 'I told you so'—"

I laughed.

"Yes, you do," I said. "You say it so often I was going to put it on a t-shirt for you."

"Oh," said mum. "Really?"

She sounded slightly hurt.

"Not really," I said. "Besides, I don't know your t-shirt size."

My mum ignored my brilliant joke and said:

"It was never going to be easy, you know that, Marcie. Working at a soup kitchen with all those homeless people."

"Mum!" I said. "They're really nice people."

"All of them?" asked my mum. "All the time?"

I let that pass. My mum worked in a pub and I have to say, from what she told me, it was about a million times worse than what I was doing.

I changed the subject.

"Mum," I said. "Do you remember someone called Louie?"

There was a pause. It felt like an odd pause for some reason.

Mum gave me the kind of look I believe people call "quizzical."

"Louie?" she repeated.

"Yes," I said. "Only tonight—"

But she wasn't listening. She was actually laughing.

"Do I remember Louie?" she said. "Do I?"

"Yes," I said, beginning to lose patience.

"I'll say I remember him," my mum said. "He was your best friend."

I stared at her. This was not the answer I had been expecting.

"What?" I said.

"Oh yes," my mum said. "You were inseparable."

"But I don't remember anyone called Louie," I said. "Come to think of it, I don't remember having a best friend. Or any friends."

My mum smiled.

"Well, that was the thing," she said. "You *didn't* have any friends."

I was getting annoyed *and* confused now.

"Mum," I said, irritated, "If I didn't have any friends, how could Louie be my best friend?"

"Easy," said Mum. "He wasn't real."

I looked at her: she had clearly lost her mind.

"What do you mean," I asked, "he wasn't real?"

Now it was her turn to look at me like I was an idiot.

"Because he was your imaginary friend," she said.

I was hopelessly confused. Imaginary friends weren't real. I mean, obviously they weren't real, they were imaginary, but also they weren't real either, in real life. People didn't have imaginary friends. Well, I didn't, anyway.

'Mum," I said. "I did not have an imaginary friend."

My mum actually snorted, like a hog.

"You absolutely did," she said. "You used to go on playdates with him, we had to talk to him and wave him goodbye, he got you presents on your birthday—"

"He what?" I said. "How did he do that if he was imaginary?"

"I don't know, I expect you bought them for yourself with your own pocket money," said my mum. She laughed. "I remember one time he even gave you a little toy cat."

"I don't remember any of this," I said.

Then my mum reached up to the shelf over my bed. The shelf was where I kept things I no longer played with: little dolls, some toy cars, that sort of thing.

"There it is," she said, and took down a tiny stuffed cat. She blew the dust off it.

"Mister Cat," I said. I put my hand over my mouth. The name had come out of nowhere.

"That was it!" said my mum. "I remember when you told us his name your dad and I couldn't stop laughing. It was probably the last thing we did laugh about together."

I looked at the little cat. Its eyes were still shiny and deep.

And I remembered.

Being in the park with Louie.

The toy in his hand. The way he looked at me.

I heard his voice again,

"It just reminded me of you," he said.

And there was something in my hand. I could see it so clearly it was like I was there again.

A toy dog.

"Dog!" I yelled. My mum leaned back, alarmed.

"His name is Dog!" I shouted. "I remember! Louie! I remember!"

And I did. I remembered everything. I remembered Louie in my room, reading his tatty old book. I remembered the Nerf gun battles. I remembered being in the park with Louie, the playground, the swings.

I remembered the day I couldn't see him anymore.

"I have to go," I told my mum.

"Go where?" she said, puzzled.

I stood up.

"Back," I said.

I ran downstairs and out of the flat, the door slamming behind me. I ran down the road, past the bus shelter, and through the park gates.

I ran along the path, towards the playground, to the place I'd last seen Louie.

I stopped.

There was a figure in front of me.

It wasn't Louie. It was large, and tattered, and hairy.

"You came back," said Tom. "You remembered."

I waved a hand at him as I tried to get my breath back. Then, when I could speak again, I said:

"Where is he?"

Tom didn't say anything.

"Where is he? Where's *Louie*?" I said, loudly. There was panic in my voice.

"He's gone back," said Tom. "Over the bridge."

For a moment I didn't understand what he meant. Then I realised.

"Is that how he came here?" I asked.

"That's how they all came here," Tom replied. "Louie, Ali—"

He stopped.

"Go home, Marcie," he said.

"No," I said. "I'm going over there. I'm going over the bridge and I'm going to find him. I'm going to find my friend."

"You can't," said Tom.

I was angry now.

"Why not?" I shouted. "He came here so I can go there!"

"That's true, in theory," said Tom. "You *can* go over the bridge."

"Then that's what I'm going to do," I said.

I stepped forward. Tom blocked my way.

"No," he said. "You don't understand."

"But I need to see him!" I said. "I remember him! He was my best friend!"

Tom took my hand.

"Listen to me, Marcie," he said. And there was something in his voice, a kind of sadness, that made me listen, even though I didn't want to.

"In this world," he said, "In our world, the one we call the real world because we're ignorant and we don't know any better, our friends—imaginary, invisible, whatever—our friends fade away when we forget them."

"I won't forget Louie again!" I said. "I promise."

"But it's the same in their world," said Tom.

I looked at him, puzzled.

"I don't understand," I said.

"Their world is just like ours," said Tom. "Ali—my friend—told me but I wasn't listening. So if they disappear from our world when we no longer believe in them—"

I suddenly got it.

"Then if we go to their world and they don't believe in us anymore—" I said.

"—we disappear," said Tom. "In their world, we only exist if they choose to believe in us. If they don't, we just fade away. Just like Ali did with me. Just like Louie did with you."

"But Louie believes in me!" I said. "He came to find me! He remembered me and he found me and—"

I stopped.

"I told him to go away," I said. "I told him I didn't remember him and I told him to go away."

Tom nodded.

"He doesn't believe in you anymore," he said. "You don't exist for him anymore. Which means if you cross that bridge and he's forgotten you, you'll fade away. For ever."

I looked at the bridge. There were, I saw, pictures on it. Faded images of people who had lost their friends because those friends—people like me—had forgotten them.

Tom must have guessed what I was thinking because he said:

"It's not fair, Marcie. But it is the way it is."

"It doesn't have to be," I said.

I got up.

"No," said Tom. "What if he's forgotten you already?"

"I have to take that chance," I said. "Because he came back for me."

And I stepped onto the bridge.

CHAPTER SEVENTEEN

The bridge was small but it felt like it took me a long time to cross it: long enough to notice that the weather was changing as I walked. On my side of the park, the weather had been—not great. A little bit grey, a little bit damp, sort of nothingy. But now, as I crossed the bridge, the sun was out, the sky was a ridiculous shade of bright blue, and I could hear birds singing and bees buzzing. It was all I could do to stop myself actually skipping across.

I restrained myself and kept walking. The other side of the park was also a contrast to my half. The grass was green and well-kept, beds of flowers were in bloom, trees grew mightily, and the playground looked like it had been opened for the first time that afternoon. Even the air was fresher. I walked around, breathing in the smells of flowers, freshly-mown grass and ice cream.

There was ice cream everywhere. Adults were eating it, kids were eating it; there was even a dog snuffling it way into a tub of something. I felt in my pocket and wondered if they used the same coins as us or would I need fairy gold or something.

There was an ice cream van parked up nearby. I walked up to it and saw a large man standing inside. He looked more like a nightclub bouncer than an ice cream man, but he seemed to be enjoying himself.

"Ice creams!" he shouted. "Get your lovely ice creams! They're very cold! With artificial flavourings!"

I couldn't help laughing. The ice cream man saw me and grinned. It was, like the rest of him, a massive grin.

"You might want to work on your sales pitch," I told him.

He beamed, revealing enormous shiny teeth like chunks of marble.

"I know!" he said. "My therapist says I need to sell myself more."

"You have a therapist?" I asked. "I've never met an ice cream man with a therapist before."

"A lot of people do," said the ice cream man solemnly. "This place may look like a sunny world of flowers and happiness, but some of us get depressed."

He beamed again.

"And you know what helps with depression?" he asked. "Ice cream!"

I nodded. He was the weirdest ice cream man I had ever met, but I liked him.

"Do you take money in this sunny world of flowers and happiness?" I asked.

"Yes I do," he said.

"Then give me a strawberry cone with a flake, please. If you have such a thing."

He looked at me. It was what people call an appraising look.

"You're not from round here, are you?" he said.

"Is it that obvious?" I replied.

"I knew it!" he said. "It's the clothes. So much black!"

I was about to point out that actually my t-shirt was a tasteful deep red when he said, excitedly, "Are you looking for someone?"

I was surprised, but then this was a surprising place.

"Yes, I am looking for someone," I told him.

"A boy. Called Louie."

The ice cream man's eyes widened which, given that they were huge already, was quite a feat.

"Louie?" he said.

"Louie," I said, nodding.

"*Louie* Louie? That Louie?" said the ice cream man again.

"I think so," I said. "Do you know him?"

He snorted like a buffalo.

"Oh yes," he said. "I'm the one who got him into this mess in the first place."

I looked at him, confused.

"What mess?" I asked.

He didn't seem to hear me.

"You're Marcie, aren't you?" he asked.

"Yes, I am," I said, excitedly. "Why, has Louie—"

"Marcie, you need to go right now," he said. "Here's your ice cream. On the house."

I ignored the strawberry cone he was holding it to me—which was hard, it looked amazing—and gave him my best tough stare.

"I'm not going anywhere," I told him.

"You have to," he said. "It's not safe."

"I know," I said. "If Louie forgets me, I'll fade away."

Now it was his turn to stare at me.

"Who told you that?" he asked.

"Tom," I replied.

He dropped the ice cream. It hit the counter with a satisfying *spudge* sound, but he didn't even notice.

"Tom?" he said in a quiet voice. "You know Tom?"

"Yes, I do," I said. "Saw him this morning, in fact."

Then it sank in.

"Wait," I said. "Are you—"

"He's over there," said Ali.

"What?" I said.

"Over there," Ali said. "Louie. Sitting on that bench with his parents. Don't turn round quickly."

I turned slowly. A few yards away there were a man and a woman, on a bench. Sitting between them, looking at his phone, was Louie.

I froze.

"I don't know what to do," I told Ali.

"You've seen him," said Ali, "Now go home. Before it's too late."

"No," I said. "I've come this far."

"You can't speak to him! You can't even let him see you!" Ali said, urgently. "Because if he doesn't believe in you—if he's given up on you—then you're done for! You're *gone*."

Ali reached out for my hand. I pulled it away.

"At least hide," he said. "Please. So he can't see you."

I thought about it.

"OK," I said.

Louie was talking to his mum and dad as I walked away from Ali and stood behind a very large tree, trying to look inconspicuous or at least like someone who liked to stand behind very large trees. I leaned over as far as I could without falling over and listened.

"I don't want to be here," Louie said.

"You can't sit in your room on your phone all day," his dad replied.

"Yes I can," said Louie, "I can sit in my room on my phone all day."

"Your dad's right," Louie's mum said.

Louie's dad looked surprised.

"See?" he said. "Even your mother agrees with me."

He breathed in like someone in a cartoon breathing in.

"All this fresh air. It'll do you good. Stop you moping."

Louie sat up and turned to him.

"Moping?" he said. "Dad, she said she didn't know me. She looked at me like I didn't exist. Like I wasn't real."

"But we aren't real to them," said Louie's mum.

"That's not true, though," Louie said. "Because once I was real to Marcie. I was real and she forgot me."

I felt terrible. Louie's face was red and angry. I wanted to step out of my hiding place. I wanted to reach out and touch Louie and say, "I'm sorry." I wanted to let him know I was there. But I held back out of guilt or fear or whatever.

And then Louie said, "Well, she's not real to me anymore."

I felt myself sway.

"That's not a nice thing to say," said Louie's mum.

"I don't care," said Louie. "She hurt me."

His dad said, "She couldn't help it, son. It's not her fault. You need to move on. You need to forget Marcie."

"That's it, Dad," said Louie, and there was something in his voice, something scary, "That's exactly what I need to do. Forget her. Wipe her from my memory."

He closed his eyes.

"I can't see her," he said.

I looked at my hand. Then I looked *through* my hand.

He covered his ears.

"I can't hear her."

I wanted to shout but I didn't have a voice.

Someone else did, though.

Ali shouted, "NO!"

Louie's parents turned. So did Louie.

"LOUIE! NO!" Ali shouted.

He pointed and Louie turned to see where he was pointing. At first Louie couldn't see me. But then the light caught me.

"Marcie?" he said.

I summoned all my strength.

"Louie—" I began.

Louie was stricken.

"Did I do this?" he asked.

He tried to touch me, but his hand went through me. Of course it did. I was air and light, nothing else.

"Marcie," Louie wailed. "I didn't mean it!"

"I know," I said.
I smiled at him to show it was all right.
And I vanished.

PART FIVE—LOUIE

CHAPTER EIGHTEEN

I made my best friend disappear. It was the worst moment of my life and it was happening to me right then. Or maybe it had just happened, or it was going to happen. I didn't know. I felt I was standing outside time, anyway. I was filled with horror at what I'd done but I couldn't move. I just stood there, looking at where Marcie had been.

I shouted:

"MARCIE!"

My dad tried to pull me away, but I pushed him back.

My mum put her hand on my shoulder.

"Leave me alone," I said.

"Louie," said my mum. "Just turn around."

I turned around.

If the park had been busy before, now it was full. There were people coming in from all directions.

And everyone was there.

My parents were there, and Ali, but also Solange and Ryan were there. And other people too, people I knew and people I didn't know. Somehow they all knew what I'd done, and they'd all come.

"Help me," I said. I didn't know who I was talking to but I said it anyway. "Help me bring Marcie back."

"She's gone, kid," said Ali.

"But I didn't mean it!" I said.

"You wanted to forget her, and you did," Ali replied.

"It was just for a second! Less than a moment!"

Ali looked at me. His eyes were sad, and sympathetic, and serious.

"That's all it takes, a moment. I'm sorry, Louie, but when you forget—you forget."

"You're wrong," said a voice. A voice I knew.

Ali turned.

Something hairy was standing behind him.

"Louie, it's a bear!" Ali shouted.

"It's me, Ali," said the bear. "And I'm not a bear."

Ali stood there for a while. He looked at Tom. He covered Tom's beard with his hand.

"Tom?" Ali said.

"Yep," said Tom.

"But how did you—how even could you—" Ali stumbled over the words. "How did you get here?"

Tom grinned.

"Easy," he said. "I came over the bridge, just like Marcie did. Because I remembered you."

He put his hand on Ali's.

"And because you never forgot me," he said.

"Tom. Ali," I said, "It's great you found each other again. But what about Marcie? She's gone."

"Is she?" asked Tom.

"Yes," said Ali. "Definitely."

Tom ignored him.

"You only forgot her for a moment, kid," he said. "Try remembering again."

I closed my eyes. I pictured her. Marcie. Laughing, smiling—fading.

"I can't," I said.

This time I screwed my eyes up. Nothing. Marcie was fading from my memory.

I started to cry. I was crying like a little kid, but I didn't care.

My dad put his arm round me. So did my mum. My friends came up and my parents made room for them. Ali put his huge arms round all of us.

"She was your best friend, Louie," Ali said.

"You loved her," said my dad.

"You'll always love her," my mum said.

"I can't breathe," said Ryan.

"Shut up, Ryan," Solange said.

I felt the warmth of their bodies against mine. I felt the way they felt about me.

And I said:

"Her name was Marcie."

Everyone stood back a little in a small circle.

"Her name was Marcie," I repeated, then corrected myself. "*Is* Marcie. She likes reading, and arguing, and shooting me with her Nerf gun. She collects toy cats. She must have a hundred but she names them all. Mister Cat. Alley Cat. Tabby Cat. Tammy Cat. Jody—"

"Ixnay on the atscay, kid," said Tom.

I looked at him, confused.

"Less cats, more Marcie," he said.

"Sorry," I said, and went on:

"She likes books about ponies and movies about killer robots. She once said that if someone made a movie called *Killer Robots Versus Cute Ponies*, she'd give them all her money. Or was it *Cute Robots Versus Killer Ponies*? It doesn't matter."

I looked at my parents and my friends.

"None of it matters," I told them. "Because Marcie is my best friend in the world and I miss her. I've missed her so much."

Everything was silent. Nothing happened.

Then someone said:

"I've missed you too, Louie."

I turned, and Marcie was there.

"Marcie?" I asked. "Is that you?"

"Of course it is," she said.

She laughed.

"Don't you know I'm unforgettable?" she said.

I grinned.

"I suppose you must be," I said.

And I hugged her.

It was one of those endless moments. You're filled with emotions and you can't speak, and it feels like it's never going to end. But that's impossible. Everything has to end.

So it was a good thing when Ali turned on the chimes in his ice cream van.

And it was an even better thing when he started giving out free ice creams.

CHAPTER NINETEEN

I could see Marcie standing on the bridge. She was looking at her watch.

"Finally," she said as I came to a halt in front of her. "I was about to slip into a coma, I've been here so long."

I didn't say. I couldn't, I was too busy trying to get my breath back.

Then Marcie said:

"Oh my goodness, Louie, what happened to you? You're drenched!"

I nodded, gulped some air into my lungs, and said:

"I know, right. It rained!"

I shook myself like a dog.

"It never rains on my side of the bridge!" I told her excitedly.

Marcie took a step back.

"All right," she said, "Remind me to tell you about umbrellas."

"I know what—"

"Never mind," she interrupted. "I've got something to show you."

I was about to follow Marcie when I noticed something.

It was the bridge.

All the photos—all the pictures—they weren't grey anymore. They weren't brown or yellow or faded.

They were brand new again.

You could see the faces of the people in them. You could see them smiling, laughing. Everyone and their friends.

"Marcie—" I said.

"I know," she said. "Come on."

We crossed the bridge and walked past the playground. People were fixing it up, painting the railings and mending the swings: even the bouncy elephants were getting new springs. The litter was gone, too, and there were fish in the lake where once there had been shopping trolleys. And—

"That's new," I said.

There was a café at the top of a small rise. It was a large tent, really, with tables and chairs, but there were people outside, and they were sitting at the tables, eating and drinking. I recognised some of them from the soup kitchen. I saw Pete and he waved at me.

"When did this happen?" I asked Marcie.

"We've been working on it a while," said Marcie. "But today's the big opening," she said.

I sniffed the air. It smelled of cakes and coffee.

"Nice job," I said.

"A lot of people helped," said Marcie.

Someone else waved. I looked over to see Tom with a woman and two children.

"You lost the beard," I said to Tom.

He smiled in fake pain.

"The kids liked it," he said. "But Sadie didn't."

"There were things living in it!" said Sadie. Then she said: "There's Ali!"

I turned to see Ali making his way hugely through the crowd.

"See you later," I said and went back to Marcie.

I looked around. I could see Solange, and Ryan, and my mum and dad, and Marcie's mum, and some random man who I guess wasn't Marcie's dad, and a whole bunch of people from my side of the park and from Marcie's side of the park.

"Wow," I said. "Is *everyone* here?"

"Not everyone," Marcie said. "Not yet."

And I saw them. A big group of people, looking lost. Marcie whistled at them. They waved and walked towards us—and kept going, into the crowd of people sitting at the tables.

My dad was the first. There was a woman in a big coat and he got out of his seat and went up to her.

"Alice?" he said.

She looked at him.

"It's me," he said. "Michael."

The woman was silent for a moment, then she said:

"*Mike?*"

My dad nodded, and he smiled in a way I'd never, ever seen him smile before.

"Yes," he said. He obviously didn't know what to say next.

"Please," he said. "Sit with us. This is my wife Sheila. Sheila, this is—"

But my mum was already standing up. A large man in a Super Mario Kart shirt was walking, almost running towards her.

"Joey?!" she said.

"Sheila?" the man in the shirt said, and almost crushed her in a hug.

It was happening all around me. People I'd never seen before were walking up to people I knew and embracing them or asking their names in disbelief or just crying. I saw a serious-looking man burst into gales of laughter as a small man with a smiling face approached him. I saw two women, one thin, one not so thin, hug each other while crying loudly. I saw grown men re-enacting clapping games and grown women skipping like lambs.

I saw Solange walk up to a kid in glasses who had a sketch pad under his arm.

"Will?" she asked. The kid ran towards her and held her tight.

I saw Ryan standing there on his own, looking sort of left out. Then someone said his name.

Ryan turned, and a tall kid with muscles on his muscles took his hand.

"Bryan?" said Ryan. "You got big, dude—aargh!"

He held up his squashed hand and they both laughed. Then to my astonishment, Ryan did a little dance. Bryan laughed and joined in.

I saw Marcie looking at me looking at Ryan and Bryan. She gave me a thumbs up.

"Looks like my work is done," she said.

"*Your* work?!" I said. Then I laughed.

"Sure thing," I said. "You did a great job, Marcie."

Marcie took a step forward. Then she hugged me.

"I love you, Louie," she said. "You are, and always have been, my best friend."

I hugged her back.

"I love you too," I told her. "I mean, probably."

"What?" she said.

"Kidding," I said.

Marcie narrowed her eyes.

"What?" I asked.

Marcie reached into her backpack.

"No," I said.

"Yes," said Marcie, pulling out the Nerf gun.

I ran.

And Marcie ran after me.

Imagine a park. A normal kind of park, same as you find in any town, with a river running right through the middle, with a bridge over it.
A perfectly normal, regular park.
That's me and Marcie's park.

THE END

ACKNOWLEDGMENTS

Major thanks to Jendia Gammon for liking this story, and thanks to Scarlett Algee for brilliant editing. And special thanks to Alexander and Laurence Quantick, who came up with some great ideas.

ABOUT THE AUTHOR

David Quantick is an Emmy Award-winning television writer, an author, movie writer, and radio broadcaster. As well as writing on *Veep*, *The Thick of It*, and *Harry Hill's TV Burp*, David also wrote the critically-acclaimed TV drama *Snodgrass*, the romantic comedy movie *Book Of Love*, and the award-winning *Whatever Happened To Baby Jane Austen?*, a Radio 4 sitcom for French and Saunders. His novel *The Hyena* is forthcoming from Stars and Sabers Publishing in November 2026.

He can be found on Bluesky at @quantick.bsky.social, on Instagram at @davidquantick, and at www.davidquantick.com.

www.ingramcontent.com/pod-product-compliance
Lightning Source LLC
LaVergne TN
LVHW041612070526
838199LV00052B/3107